WET DREAMS FOR OLDIES 1

NEVER FEEL LONELY AGAIN

ANONYMOUS

A book must be the axe for the frozen sea within us.

FRANZ KAFKA

CONTENTS

ONE

THE TEA LADY

Elsa loved Monday's. It was the day she didn't wear her knickers at work. Monday was the day nearly half of all her customers in the twenty offices on her two floors at the top of a Sydney skyscraper, worked from home.

But on Mondays, a relaxed Elsa was the busiest woman in the building.

Elsa was born in France to a wealthy couple and christened Eloise Binoche.

Her father was from a well-off family of importers and her mother had been a servant girl in the large Binoche home, and, as Eloise discovered later, Antoinette had also been a sex worker before she joined the staff at the Binoche mansion.

When her parents realised how intelligent their daughter was, Eloise was enrolled at the Sorbonne where she studied mathematics. Her lessons were taught in English and after a few years and proving herself an outstanding student, Eloise found herself living in New York working as a systems analyst for a prestigious Wall Street investment firm.

After both parents died a few years later, Eloise discovered that her inheritance would be sufficient to keep her in luxury for a lifetime and she pondered her future and what she wanted from life.

At university, Eloise had discovered that she enjoyed men's company and when she settled overseas, she managed to satisfy herself reasonably well with suitors from the large number of males working in her profession.

But Eloise felt that there was something missing in her life and in a sudden fit of imaginative reflection, she realised that, of her loving parents, it was her mother's past life she most admired, in particular her little known days as a sex worker.

Eloise found her mother's diary and studied the faded written pages in the old cloth-bound notebook.

Antoinette didn't offer much in the way of helpful hints for sex workers, but in her final sentences she mentioned a friend who was a very successful older woman. She mentioned that Fayette was a follower of the little known "soft and slow method" and that she always had customers.

Eloise was intrigued and so wished that her mother had left more than this brief note. What was this soft and slow method?

As happens, Eloise had only recently joined a yoga class. Kundalini Yoga For Sexual Energy & Power was a class offered in a building close to where she worked so her interest was doubly piqued when she noticed "Slow Sex" being offered as an optional component in the information on the website. Could this help Eloise understand what the successful prostitute, Fayette, practiced?

Eloise arranged to meet her teacher for a one-on-one discussion and hopefully discover more about slow sex.

"Slow sex was practiced by many of the older concubines of the harem. It suited their older and slower bodies and it was much appreciated by experienced males. It is very different to the more energetic sex that most people experience and it is said that with genuine slow sex, peoples orgasms are superior."

Eloise was much taken with what her female master yoga practitioner, Mira, told her. She was even more excited when the yogini smiled and reached forward and took Eloise's hand and in a low voice, suggested she might like to come to the school on a Monday evening after classes finished and practise the slow art with a few other students.

"And best you don't wear any knickers. It helps with your mood and expectations and it certainly makes things easier for everyone."

Eloise was excited and looked forward to discovering what seemed to be the method of choice of her mother's friend all those years ago.

Eloise joined two women and three men in a semi-darkened room at her yoga school one evening after classes had finished.

It was so exciting when she was told to reach forward and gather the loose testicles and cock in her hand of the man standing in front of her and to just hold them, moving her fingers only slightly to acknowledge its softness.

Eloise was instructed to let the cock lay on her open hand while she gently fingered it using only her finger tips and to occasionally touch the bulbous head of it with her thumb.

A little while after that, she was told to close her fingers around it and hold it with only a semblance of pressure from the fingers spread along its length.

Every so slowly, the cock grew bigger in her hand and Eloise wondered what she should do next.

Feeling the tiny responses and becoming aware of the cock in her hand slowly increasing in size was truly exciting and it was all Eloise could do to hold back and not offer more energetic encouragement.

Eloise went on to discover that small finger movements and gentle caressing along with certain ways of holding a penis or a vulva, led to an ecstatic state of being and eventually, to an enhanced orgasm.

But that was not the only excitement on offer. Her teacher told the three couples to stand in a triangle, the women on the inside and with a man standing in front of each of them.

Then, as a women fondled a man with her right hand, each reached between the legs of the woman on her left with her free hand and cupped a full handful of vagina and, following instructions, gently and slowly fondled it with her finger tips.

A murmur of excitement was heard when Pricilla, the woman that Eloise had only just began to fondle and while she was considering whether or not she should let her index finger follow the wet and slippery path between the woman's labia lips, yelled "Yes" and immediately orgasmed, shuddering and causing the man she was fondling to push forward and also yell out.

Everyone agreed that the lesson had been most informative as well as enjoyable to which their teacher replied that they were of course, free to practice with whom and whenever they wanted too, but if they wished, they could repeat the lesson each Monday at around 9pm.

Everyone agreed to do this, saying that the more practice the better, and all looked forward to touching each other on Monday nights.

If there was an obvious difference between the men and women, it was the men's lack of interest in touching each other. The younger man, Brendan signalled that he didn't really have a problem with it but the lack of interest from the other two meant that it didn't happen.

The women, on the other hand, showed immediate interest in touching each other, even the seemingly repressed and self proclaimed virginal Pricilla signalled her willingness with a smile that seemed bigger than her face. Her orgasmic outburst earlier when Eloise had touched her had put slow sex on her agenda permanently.

The six met weekly for eight week and in that time, Eloise proved beyond any shadow of doubt that this was the path for her.

In the tumultuous months that followed her initiation into the gentle arts of slow sex, Eloise questioned her life constantly.

One evening her thoughts and emotions came to a head and she set about changing everything. She quit her job and in just weeks, Eloise found herself living in a very comfortable apartment in Australia's premier city with a view over the long curving sandy beach of Bondi.

But before departing for Sydney, Eloise made a dash to London to shop and then moved on to Paris where she visited the family solicitor and also her preferred shoe shop where a matronly staff member double checked the measurements of her feet so that Eloise could continue to order her footwear on line.

Change or no change, Eloise's shoes would always be a priority.

When her Australian neighbour mentioned that her husband had complained that his firm's tea lady was about to retire after twenty-four years of service, Eloise had another moment of awakening, realising that this was exactly the opportunity she needed.

How better to change her life than to become a tea lady.

Her smart good looks and near perfect english established Eloise's bonafide except she did have to make and pour a cup of tea for the managing director, the ageing Mr Bradley.

Her intelligent foresight had seen Eloise making many cups of tea at home for her Aussie neighbours before the interview and on the day, her tea making abilities proved more than satisfactory.

Mr Bradley was the one remaining original founder of Morgan Industries. He was in his late eighties and never took any interest in hiring and firing, except for the most important position in the company; the tea lady.

At Eloise's interview with the venerable gentleman, when she bent over to retrieve the biscuit tin from the bottom shelf of her tea trolly and she felt Mr Bradley's fingers gently exploring her stocking seams all the way down the back of her legs to her ankles, she took her time while straightening up. And instead of turning, Eloise looked back over her shoulder and with a special smile which suggested she was happily complicit in Mr Bradley's leg touching adventure, asked, "Would you like one biscuit or two, Mr Bradley?"

Eloise never did get to meet the outgoing tea lady. She expected that the rumoured crabby Mrs Simm would show her the ropes for the first few days but that was not to be. Instead, she accompanied the pleasant Mrs Symons, the tea lady for level nineteen for three days and quickly learnt what was required.

Eloise was impressed with Mrs Symons relaxed and unflustered manner, even under sometimes difficult circumstance. Sometimes people were in a bad mood. Others might have a number of visitors who all wanted something different.

Anything could be happening behind the door she tapped on before wheeling in her trolly.

"You will see everything, darling. But nothing fazes me anymore," Mrs Symons said in a quiet voice. The smartly dressed older woman looked at Eloise. "Sometimes it can get quite steamy so I hope for your sake you're not too much of a prude. And I can see by looking at you that you will attract attention from the men and from the women."

Eloise wanted to ask Mrs Symons more about what the word steamy meant. But then she was rewarded when the lovely lady read her thoughts and provided answers.

"I'm a woman on my own so I can do whatever I like, if you know what I mean. I've always enjoyed sex. Some of the older men here fancy me and often I like them. I get offers. This will happen to you, darling, rest assured.

"I do play but I have my rules. Firstly they must be made to pay, if only to prove they appreciate me. A $20 note tucked into the top of my stocking signals a hand job is desired. Two $20's indicate a blow job, and a $50 means I'll bend over the trolly and pull down my knickers and wriggle my rear end and they get my pussy for five minutes.

"Keeping things simple is very important. Oh, and I make sure I carry a tube of lube."

Eloise was in awe of Mrs Symons forthright approach to life, or more particularly, to those things that can be referred to what Eloise now understood as "steamy". She mumbled a "Thank you for that essential lesson, Mrs Symons. Forewarned, as you say."

In bed that night, Eloise could not but think about Mrs Symons advice. She had confirmed what Eloise had suspected, that sexual interactions could be on her terms and she could enjoy exactly what she had hoped for.

Sufficient to say that Eloise's repertoire of moves designed to impress men included basic things like wearing stockings with seams, bending forward in a certain way and of course the ultimate winning move, a smile that promised a man the possibility of going directly to heaven.

Eloise's successful handling of Mr Bradley's morning and afternoon deliveries ensured that she would have her job for life, or at least for duration of Mr Bradley's working lifetime.

Eloise rebranded herself as Elsa feeling that name more easily expressed her tea-lady persona.

Everyone loved the new tea lady. For a week or two, Elsa was mentioned regularly whenever staff met up. "She sure is a sexy bit of stuff," commented the men, and "She's so stylish. Its said she's part French. That would explain a lot. And the shoes ...?" said the women.

Elsa was now officially a tea lady and the controller of the beautiful old Art Nouveau chrome and glass trolly and everything on it. She was mistress of her own little boat, sailing the corridors and the lift between twenty different countries and people. She sailed under an independent flag, protected by the man at the top, a now fully provided for and besotted Mr Bradley.

Monday was the day many of her tea or coffee customers on her two floors at the top of the city skyscraper, didn't come into the office. Instead of ten offices on each of two floors being occupied, Monday's saw this number reduced by half, if not more.

Most took the day off for an extended weekend choosing to work from home. Secretaries would sometimes come into the office to catch up on their work in a peaceful atmosphere free of the demands of their bosses.

Excessive weekend indulgence or simply wanting to extend their weekend holiday, meant that heading into the city was the last thing they wanted to do.

Monday was the quiet day at Morgan Industries. And it was the day Elsa was most appreciated. It was the day when Elsa, for different reasons, became the busiest woman in the place.

After discovering and embracing the soft and slow method as her sexual creed, Elsa was now intent on happily pursuing anything pertaining to finding or satisfying her desire for sexual encounters. Like so many faith based activities, following "the path" led to its own rewards and satisfaction.

Elsa wished no one any harm and she planned to carefully welcome everyone who sought to enjoy her and her ways of behaving. Elsa would provide slow sensual leadership. Most times, sexual activities suffered from the fumbling attempts that comes with a desperate rush to achieve gratification.

Elsa believed firmly that soft and slow ultimately wins the day and gives everyone what they needed.

Elsa planned her new work life with great precision.

First she needed to consolidate her relationship with Mr Bradley. This was not difficult to achieve.

From Mr Bradley's first moments of his touching the backs of Elsa's legs, it was only around a week later that he happily watched the smiling tea lady hold and fondle his penis in a loving fashion. At the same time, she placed one of his hands gently but firmly on the soft moist hairy and welcoming wet spot between her legs and at that moment the most powerful man in the organisation become Elsa's willing sex slave. Morgan Industries happy octogenarian CEO would never object to whatever enjoyment Elsa was offering.

Elsa savoured this moment of seduction and the feelings that accompanied her activities. She totally owned her bosses cock and pleasuring him pleasured her too. The tiny spasms that issued via Mr Bradley's prostate glands echoed faintly through Elsa's body and knowing that both he and she were lovingly enjoying themselves was Elsa's ultimate reward.

The top floor of ten senior managers' offices provided Elsa with ten likely customers - mostly men but some female - and most of whom had an adjoining room housing a secretary - mostly women but occasionally a man. This provided her with around twenty tea or coffee drinkers, most of whom she would visit twice a day. And as Elsa was later to discover, there were often visitors from other parts of the building or elsewhere in the city.

Elsa planned that the first week or two would be for reconnaissance only but things could often get confusing and even challenging for the new tea lady's plans.

Elsa hadn't foreseen just how horny these people were and how easily they responded to a smart looking women in conservative clothing and who happened to wear stockings and medium heels.

Men and women came onto her constantly and she found herself smiling and conveniently blushing and repeating the phrase. "Thank you, but please let me have a week or two to settle in. I've only been here a few days and I need to learn the ropes."

Most times it was accepted in good faith. It also gave Elsa the opportunity to catalogue her tea lady customers and sift through those candidates she would eventually go looking for when Elsa decided she could enjoy herself in the way she wanted.

Elsa was pleasantly surprised by what was on offer.

From the shy but sexy Mr Allan in No. 3 who remarked on her beautiful footwear; the bitch goddess in No.8, surrounded by adoring females, immediately suggesting that Elsa take off her clothes and let her girls have some fun with her; or the red faced lion tamer type in No. 10 who simply asked when Elsa would be up for it and what dollar value notes did he need to keep in his desk drawer?

The future for Elsa's desire for slow sex looked promising but also challenging.

After three weeks in the job, Elsa chose Mondays to be her "no knickers day" and start her hopefully, erotic adventures.

Elsa chose the manager in No.3 as her first assignment.

"You're looking as beautiful as ever, Elsa."

"Thank you Mr Allen. And I'm rating you as the best looking man on Floor Twenty. And, of all the managers, I bet you also have the most beautiful partner at home? Now! Tea! Black with one sugar. Am I right?"

Elsa's smile was captivating and she was hopeful of a positive outcome.

Mr Allen watched attentively as Elsa bent down to open the biscuit box. Not only was she without her knickers, she had also worn a shorter skirt than usual.

Elsa could feel Mr Allen's gaze and wondered how much of her was on display. Then she felt him lifting up her hem and Elsa knew instinctively that her ship was probably going to set sail and she felt a tiny shiver of excitement.

Then Mr Allen cupped Elsa's warm damp vagina in his hand and squeezed it lovingly.

"Oh, Mr Allen, I sense you are feeling very loving towards me. Are you sure that this is what you want, you darling man? Are you simply playing or would you like me to feel your cock?

"Monday is a very quiet day. It's when I can enjoy a slower and more intimate pace of working and fit in other things. Please feel free to play with me. And may I return the pleasure?"

Elsa turned and swiftly reached for the lump in Mr Allen's pants. In moments she had his substantial cock in the palm of her hand and with her thumb and fingers, she gently squeezed it. Elsa wore her angelic smile, assuring him that this was exactly what they both should be doing.

"Lets enjoy this moment Mr Allen. And I must just say that you have a very beautiful cock. I love it."

Elsa turned and bent over her trolly then she introduced Mr Allen's cock into her welcoming vagina and in a soft voice, asked the man to please enjoy her slippery heavenly offering in a slow moving way.

Elsa surrendered to this first sexual encounter, celebrating the beginning of her new sensual working life.

Mr Allen eventually let out a yell and filled Elsa with his cum. Then he fell back into his office chair and slumped smiling at her as she turned and lovingly returned his cock to his underpants and zipped his trousers.

"Thank you Mr Allen. That was lovely. Now I must tell you now that I'm very happy to provide this service at any time you feel you want me. However, there will be a small charge." Elsa went on to repeat Mrs Symons list of charges.

"A $20 note tucked into the top of my stocking means that you would like a hand job. Two $20's means a blow job is preferred, and a $50 entitles you to bend me over the trolly and I'll pull down my knickers and you can have my pussy for five minutes, or in your case, Mr Allen, we might enjoy it for little longer.

"Most times I can give immediate service, but if for some reason I'm in a hurry, I'll get back to you later in the day."

Elsa leant forward and kissed Mr Allen then turned to leave.

"Thank you Elsa. That was wonderful. I will be stuffing your stocking tops regularly."

It didn't take Elsa long to discover the truth of what made office life swing.

Friday nights was when people stayed back at work. It was an extra late shift and overtime for Elsa, but she didn't mind. And she soon discovered that many, if not most of the staff stayed back for reasons other than work.

This revelation started when she knocked and entered the office of one of the directors on a Friday evening. What she was confronted with made her hesitate and think she that she should leave. But then Mr Ferguson called out to her to come in.

"It's all right, Elsa. I'm sure you've met Ms Stanton, my secretary. She likes to relax at the end of the week."

Elsa stared at the woman kneeling in front of Mr Ferguson. Elsa had visited her in her own office next door, earlier in the day and vividly remembered the woman commenting on Elsa's shoes and stockings and asking her to bend over to give her a better look.

Just like Mr Bradley, the week before, Ms Stanton reached out and ran her fingers up and down Elsa's legs, commenting that with legs like that, she thought Elsa would do very well in this job.

Now Ms Stanton was on the carpet minus her dress and looking like the perfect bimbo slut in her french underwear. Her legs were lazily waving from side to side and her red painted toenails showing from the ends of her Italian strappy heels, stamped the woman as the perfect upperclass office whore as she calmly stroked and sucked her bosses cock, flashing her bright eyes at him to ensure he felt special.

Elsa acted unfazed and set about serving them both with tea. As she did so, Ms Stanton stopped sucking and looked up and smiled. "Two sugars, thanks Elsa," then she continued with her Friday night relaxing routine.

Elsa smiled and murmured "certainly" and "thank you" and a "goodbye" and quietly left the office. A cup of tea was the only thing she would be offering Mr Ferguson today.

Elsa pushed her trolly to No.8 and knocked and entered. Silvia Bender sat behind her desk and didn't look up as Elsa entered.

Since their first chaotic introduction which resulted in Elsa simply leaving the office, Elsa had discovered that she really liked Silvia and that she was a super intelligent and loving woman, probably in her late-thirties and worshipped by the two older women who occupied desks nearby.

"I just don't know what came over me when we first met, Elsa" she had later whispered, apologetically. "I suspect it's early onset of menopause. My girls are helping me through it."

Elsa took hold of Silvia's hand and said simply. "I'm definitely up for a romp with you and your girls, any time, Silvia. But I am fully committed to slow and sensitive interactions. Please get in touch if you need me. Monday is my best time because its very quiet around here. But I'm available at short notice most days."

Silvia smiled and looked lovingly at Elsa. "Thank you Elsa, I appreciate it. And I know you will enjoy Margaret and Prudence. They've both indicated that they would love to get their head between your thighs. But they don't work full time." Then Silvia's smile widened. "I'm sure I will want you too, Elsa but it might have to be solo. Can I text you sometime soon?"

Elsa handed Silvia a piece of paper with her mobile number written on it.

"Solo sounds wonderful and hopefully it will be sooner rather than later? And who knows, it might be what a busy girl needs right now?"

"Yes, Elsa. I will want you very soon!"

Elsa wasn't planning to rush into anything much with the lion tamer type man in No. 10. But the more she served Mr Bountiful - yes that was his real name - tea and biscuits, the more interesting he became.

He was certainly overtly interested in her but he maintained a respectful distance and Elsa appreciated his kind and controlled response to her. Yes, he wanted to know her better, but he was obviously prepared to wait.

It was almost as though he was sure she would favour him in the not too distant future and he was happy to play along.

It was a clever strategy and it was working. It made Elsa more excited at the prospect of offering him her services and this rarely was the case with others, at least to the degree she found herself getting hot when each time she entered his office and served Mr B his tea and biscuit.

The day came when Elsa decided to tell Mr Bountiful what she was offering. She was nervous as she entered his office and began pouring his usual weak black tea to be served with one biscuit.

"Mr Bountiful? I have information for you relating to something you asked me about when we first met."

Mr B looked up from his desk. "Indeed? Please continue, Elsa."

"You might or perhaps might not recall asking me if I would be up for it. Well, I've had time to settle in and I can now inform you that I am making myself available to a select few and that there will be a charge."

Before Elsa could continue, Mr B asked a question.

"More than once a week, Elsa?"

"Yes, Mr Bountiful, as many times as you wish to pay me for. And I should explain that you simply need to put a fifty dollar note into my stocking top each time you wish to secure my services."

Mr Bountiful stared at Elsa in anticipation.

"I should also inform you that I am a follower of the slow method of sexual enjoyment and will not respond to rough play or overly demonstrative sexual endeavours."

Elsa stopped speaking and turned back to tidy her trolly before leaving. When she turned to smile and say thank you and goodbye, Mr Bountiful was on his feet with a fifty dollar note in his hand. He stepped over to her and lifted the front of her skirt and slid the folded bill into her stocking top.

Elsa stared back at her new suitor and smiled. Then she reached forward and put her hand on his trouser front.

"Thank you, Mr Bountiful. I've been looking forward to this moment."

Elsa began to release Mr B's cock from its cage. She gave an excited little shiver as the man lifted her skirt and gently slid his hand between her legs to take possession of her warm moist hairy pussy.

The two kissed slowly as Elsa laid Mr B's fast growing cock across the palm of her hand. Then she closed her fingers around it and began a slow squeezing moment in response to Mr B's throbbing member.

When Elsa had enjoyed the feelings she received from playing with Mr B's cock and judged it time to move on, she looked at the happy man and murmured "front or back?"

Mr B looked lovingly at Elsa. "Your back end today, Elsa, I'll look forward to having you from the front tomorrow."

Ignoring her own rules, Elsa leant forward and kissed Mr B on the lips, Then she turned and leant over her trolly and lifted her skirt up and tucked it into her waist band.

The two came together perfectly. Mr B shagged Elsa gently but firmly and she savoured the sensations in her vagina. Then she felt the whole of Mr B's body stiffen as he ejaculated, depositing a large amount of cum into her welcoming house of happiness.

Elsa reached down and pulled up her knickers. Then she turned and put Mr B's cock in her mouth, lovingly sucking her juices and his from his retreating member.

"Thank you, Mr Bountiful. I really enjoyed that. It was much appreciated."

Mr Bountiful looked at her adoringly.

"Are you married, Elsa?"

As Elsa reached to open the door, she looked back. "No, Mr Bountiful! This way is my preferred *modus operandi*. It's far less complicated and I'm sure that you will appreciate my services much more than if I was your wife."

Silvia from No. 8 messaged Elsa and asked if she would be available during the week. Her girls, Margaret and Prudence would be in on Wednesday and Thursday so that it would be good if she could make it on either of those days. Call me, Elsa and I'll fill you in a little more on the girls. They have a kink.

Elsa managed to phone Silvia later in the day telling her that either day would be suitable, and also, what should she know about their kink?

"Well, darling I'm not quite sure how to tell you. As you know they are both in their early fifties and both have a huge experience with love and life. I love them dearly and they always manage to give me a good time when they think I'm getting a bit stressed.

"Anyway, in conversation, they both admitted to being cum queens in the past and, given the opportunity, happy to lay back and get filled up at any time in the future.

"Moving quickly on, it turns out that they both also love licking and sucking each other after a cum queen event. I'm telling you just incase you could see your way to visit us after you've had a moment with a man who gives you a cream pie and which you would happily share with Margaret and Prudence. What are your thoughts, Elsa?"

It didn't take Elsa long to reply. Thursdays was a day when she could be reasonably certain she would welcome at least two contributions from men. She told Silvia that she could visit her late in the day, at around 4.30 and be reasonably sure she could provide her girls with a cream pie treat.

"Oh you are such a darling. They will love you for ever. We'll expect you on Thursday and around 4.30. I'm sure they will be eagerly awaiting you.

It was Thursday and Elsa headed towards Silvia's office. Not only had she received cream pies from Mr Allen and Mr Ferguson. Mr Allen had a friend visiting at lunch time and it took very little to persuade the friend that he should try this fabulous tea lady.

After much stuffing of money into Elsa's stocking top, both men took turns in stuffing Elsa, both agreeing that this tea lady was surely the best in the land.

Elsa loved their attention and when they each blew their load, Elsa orgasmed stronger than usual and turned and sucked them and told them what a lucky tea lady she was to enjoy such beautiful cocks.

Elsa wasn't sure what happened but suddenly they had both regained their erections and bent her back over her trolly and each gave it to her again, coming almost as strongly the second time as the first and giving Elsa a second orgasm.

Mr Allen smiled down at Elsa. "I think we owe you for a second round, Elsa?"

Elsa gave them both her most loving smile.

"This girl has been well paid in kind gentlemen. No further payment is needed. Now I must flee as I'm running just a little late. Thank you both. I loved it!"

When Elsa entered Silvia's office, she locked the door. Taking Elsa's hand and telling her to leave her trolly behind, she led her into the back room where Margaret and Prudence were already on a bed feeling each other between the legs. Elsa looked at them and thought what a sexy couple of sluts they were.

"I've bought you a present, girls. How would you like it?"

In a split second, Margaret moved Elsa onto the bed and she and Prudence pushed her backwards and dragged her legs apart. Then, with their heads taking turns between her thighs, the two licked and sucked the enormous amount of liquid flowing from Elsa's vagina while Elsa lay with her eyes closed loving the attention she was getting.

After a few minutes, Margaret and Prudence turned and looked up adoringly at Silvia who was almost in a trance staring at what was going on.

"Come and join us, boss. There is plenty for everyone. Elsa has had a busy afternoon by the look of it."

Silvia looked unsure, but then surrendered to her companions and they cheered as she put out her tongue and licked up the juices slowly dribbling from Elsa.

Elsa smiled at Silvia and her companions and told them that she hoped they could all do this more often.

Silvia sat back on her heels and looked at her companions. "I think we can manage to do that, don't you, girls?"

"Yes, boss. We would love to do this again."

TWO

PEDRO

It was mid morning on Monday and Mary had just started work as a receptionist at The Pines, a private hotel in a beautiful mansion and grounds in the Blue Mountains, just west of Sydney.

Leanne, the regular office manager who was leaving for overseas in a few days, was showing Mary what was required of her in her daily routine.

Mary tried to concentrate on all of what Leanne was showing her.

"Booking people in as they arrive is obviously an important part of the job."

"Because we are pet friendly, guests mostly know to leave their pets in the car until you have finished checking them in and you've handed them the keys of their unit. Then they are advised that they can deliver their pets to the kennels and the kennel maids."

"Telephone enquiries probably comes second. Many calls will be from people wanting to book ahead or make changes to bookings."

"What else? Oh yes! Now we keep these under the counter but guests know to ask for them."

Leanne lifted a tray of sex toys up onto the counter and Mary woke up with a start.

"Most people bring their own with them but it is surprising how many we sell, especially this one."

Leanne held up a multicoloured bubble shaped model. The back end was shaped for insertion into the vagina of the wearer.

Mary ventured to ask if there was also a strap-on model.

"There is but no one asks for them. Our guests are wanting to fantasise and capture a special feeling and they all claim that this model ensures they feel everything. You can see that there is a small finger of soft fine rubber at the back which rubs against the clitoris when in action. It's a lot of fun to use."

She passed it to Mary who gingerly took it her hand and inspected it.

Leanne went over the office tasks. Booking diary, receipt books, correct telephone answering messages etcetera. Then she showed Mary the electronic security system and told her what should be done if there was an emergency.

Mary found herself looking closely at the woman she was going to stand in for as she bent down over the filing cabinet. She wondered what it would be like to make love to her and tried to visualise what she would look like in just her underwear. Leanne had such a shapely arse as did Mary and Mary could smell the woman's subtle perfume. And yet her clothing spoke of an ordinary housewife living an ordinary life. Maybe Leanne was married?

Mary now found herself looking closely at almost everyone she met and she enjoyed these fantasy moments.

Going to the recently opened female friendly club close to where she lived had broken down all barriers to exploring other peoples lives and loves. Her experience at The Club, along with the intense sexual feelings that Mary had recently experienced had changed her life and so far, she had no regrets.

Mary had at first been worried about her new found horniness and consulted her doctor about the hormone treatment she was receiving.

Doctor Meg had assured her that the dose was minimal and should not be affecting her in any way.

"It must be something else going on," she answered with a smile. "Best you simply learn to enjoy it."

Leanne and Mary were sitting in the small lounge accessible either through the door in the corridor marked Private or directly through a door at the back of reception. It was Mary's fifth day at The Pines.

The office would close from 2 pm until 5 pm which was the time when most guests were enjoying dalliances with their friends in their rooms. The office would reopen for two hours at five o'clock.

It was Leanne's final week before her vacation.

"Tell me about the other staff members, Leanne. Is there anything I need to know for reasons to do with my role in the office?"

"Ah yes! That is important."

Leanne settled back with her tea and biscuit.

"Well, firstly, the kennel maids, Charlotte and Fiona are very important members of the crew."

"They know everything about the guests and their pets."

"Charlotte trained as a vet so is the goto person for all pet health problems. She also does massage; both pets and people."

"Fiona comes from a sheep farming background and is a wizard at dog training."

Leanne stopped talking to catch a soggy biscuit that she had dunked.

Mary studied the lovely Leanne more closely. There were things she wanted to know about her.

"Do you have a pet, Leanne, if you don't mind me asking."

Leanne gave Mary a knowing smile.

"Well, not really. But we do have a pretend Miniature Dachshund. My husband, Dean, was on a business trip to Bangkok and discovered something he'd never seen before and bought it for me, or should I say, for us. It's a wireless operated vibrator hidden inside a soft toy. Dean or I can operate it from our smart phones."

"We've called it Pedro and it's certainly added something special to our sex life. Dean is a wonderful lover and he keeps me more than happy. But in the last couple of months we've added Pedro into our bedroom fun."

"One of my favourite positions is riding cowgirl on top of Dean and he loves it too."

"One Sunday afternoon, a week or two after we first got Pedro, Dean asked me to lean forward over his chest and as I did so he reached under the pillow and brought out the squeegee of lube and proceeded to add lube to my anus. Then he smiled at me and reached over to the bedside table and gathered Pedro up and gently laid the toy sausage dog between my buttocks, adjusting its position close to my special spot."

"We had not at this stage tried the toy, thinking it was probably a bit of a gimmick. The vibrator part was a nice clear plastic and looked quite solid and serious. I giggled and reached behind me and adjusted it so that the knob of the pretend cock rested against my freshly lubed bum hole. Then Dean put his hand firmly on top of Pedro to stop it falling off.

"I lay still thinking Dean was being silly and playful. Moments later I let out a gasp and a scream as Dean activated Pedro. The vibrator pushed easily into my well lubed bum and moments later it was sliding in and out and giving me the anal shagging of a lifetime."

"Dean immediately pushed up his cock and increased his efforts from under me and I found myself heaving my body and synchronising the two of them. It was delicious."

"Eventually we both came at the same time and this girl experienced her closest-to-heaven moment. Since then, Pedro usually gets a go at me on most Sundays.

"The great thing about it is that as long as we keep a supply of batteries on hand it could keep humping my willing bum all afternoon. We call it our going to toy-land.

"Dean loves it as much a I do because it increases my pussy pressure on his cock. He also loves experimenting with the settings. I think we've tried them all: fast, medium, slow, and vibrate, and intermittent and smooth."

Leanne paused to finish her chocolate biscuit.

"I've never told anyone about it except you so I would appreciate it if you didn't mention it to anyone, Mary. Some things you just like to keep to yourself, especially in a place like this where I'm so much in the public eye."

Mary was impressed with Leanne's story and it also made her feel distinctly horny.

"You are a sexy looking woman Leanne. Do guests come onto you? I know I jolly well would."

Mary laughed.

"Can I take that as a compliment from another sexy looking woman? And to answer the question, yes, all the time and it's a lot of fun.

"You will be propositioned endlessly, Mary. I can see that. But always feel free to give a big smile and say, 'thank you but no thank you' or 'maybe at another time' unless of course the offer looks so good that you feel the urge to put yourself out there immediately."

Mary blushed and laughed.

"Often, I entertain ladies here in this room.

"My nickname is the Anal Angel, and I give it to them with a small dildo. My experience with our mechanical Pedro has provided me with extra experience so that no one ever goes away disappointed.

"They usually book me the day before and often they come with a friend. I love it. Dragging down their knickers and pulling them backwards on top of me on this arm chair and giving it to their bum while I finger their pussy is very exciting. Their companions all love it too, watching me giving it to their girlfriend gets them excited. Often they will finger each other while I'm looking after the back end. And they always want to smother me with kisses.

"Watching while someone else is getting a good anal shafting is very exciting for these mainly country women who so rarely have another human to share erotic experiences with, other than when they are on holidays, here at The Pines."

Mary glanced at the clock. There was still a bit more than an hour to go before they lifted the shutters and reopened the kiosk.

"Leanne, if it is a really quiet day and you have no suitors, what do you do for three hours?"

"Well, occasionally I'll head off to the Mall and shop. Sometimes I'll catch up on reading. I'm in a bookclub. Other times, well, I'll head upstairs to our staff apartment and just settle back and play with myself."

Both women laughed loudly.

"So Leanne, if a girl needed help with her anal experience so that she can better serve the guests while you are away, would she ask you for help? I'm hot to trot and would love to learn more."

Mary smiled and stood up and went to the bottom draw of the desk and got out a small dildo.

"I thought you'd never ask, Mary. This would be a good time for you to practise and also for you to see the office manager's apartment. Let's head upstairs where we can canoodle. I want my head up your skirt and your fingers on my pussy. Lets go and get slutty."

The two women came together like old lovers rekindling a flame. Knickers came off and tops and bras magically opened and the mouths of two lusty women fed on one another while their hands played games in the knowledge that they would soon happily orgasm.

When each woman came, the sounds were pure and loud and each body shook.

Leanne looked down on the happy Mary.

"Pity I'm going away, Mary. I could happily invite you around to do that again. And you would love my darling Dean's lovely cock."

"Now, slut! Stand up and lean over the back of the sofa and let me pop in some lube. We had better start your anal training."

Leanne caressed and licked Mary 's buttocks as she gently pushed them apart and squeegeed the lube into the special spot. Then she inserted the back end of the dildo into her vagina and told Mary to be ready.

"I'm very ready, Leanne. Please do it."

Mary couldn't remember ever having the feelings she felt after Leanne slipped the dildo into her anus. It wasn't like having vaginal sex.

The smooth, soothing feel of the rubber thingy sliding leisurely backwards and forwards in her bottom made Mary feel both relaxed and excited at the same time. She wanted to simply fade away into a dream world but she also wanted to swing herself over and fasten her mouth on Leanne's large well-formed rear end.

"Oh, Leanne, this is heavenly. I want it to go on for ever. You are so good at this. And I can't help thinking about your Pedro,"

Leanne gave a momentary hard thrust of her abdomen.

"You voluptuous slut! I hoped you would be thinking about my beautiful lonely bum and what you desperately wanted to do to it, that is if I can be persuaded to let you near it."

"Tell me you want to fuck my bottom, you randy bitch. I don't let just any attractive woman stick a rubber cock into my delicate derriere."

Mary wriggled with excitement.

"Oh yes, Leanne. Yes, yes! I desperately want to fuck you. But give me a bit more first. I want you to satisfy my cravings for it."

They swapped positions and Mary rubbed her hands over Leanne's back and shoulders. Then she took a large buttock in each hand and squeezed them, then she added lubricant on her pink anus before she thrust the rubber cock into Leanne's welcoming rear.

The two women came at the same time and slumped onto the carpet. Leanne gasped and uttered oaths expressing her pleasure and Mary took deep breaths and moved to lean against the sofa.

"I think you are going to enjoy working here, Mary. And I bet you'll be availing yourself of the ladies fantasy afternoons the first time they make you an offer. You're a beautiful slut and the residents will be lining up for your favours."

The two rested and then Leanne turned and looked at Mary.

"Now I think I want to give you another turn, darling. Here, open your legs and let me pop this in."

Leanne's fingers deftly opened Mary's vagina and inserted the givers end of the rubber dildo. Then she looked into Mary's eyes and leant forward and kissed her lovingly on the mouth, cupping her breasts and flicking her fingers across Mary's hard nipples.

Leanne squeezed some lube onto her fingers and reached back to apply it between her cheeks.

"Now, you sexy new office manager, let my rear-end have your full attention."

Leanne turned on her knees and pushed back towards Mary who responded with loving caresses and licking of the woman's large bottom. Then she moved in with the dildo and suddenly, she found herself dealing out what she had received only moments ago.

Having Leanne's beautiful buttocks slapping gently against her belly was divine. And the tiny soft rubber finger at the end of the dildo was like magic on Mary's clit. Mary found herself trembling with excitement.

"Oh Leanne , you feel so beautiful. I don't think I'll ever be able to stop."

"That is fine by me, my darling slut. You can fuck me like this forever. I'm loving it."

Leanne was taking off two months to holiday with her husband. She spent a couple of hours showing Mary a map of the layout of The Pines. The lovely lady was determined that she know as much about the place as possible for when she started as relieving receptionist, the following week.

"Now for the good bits! Oops! Did I say that?"

The two woman laughed and Mary yelled, "At last!"

"Within the property, much happens that would probably interest a liberated woman."

"The Pines is noted for its wholesome farm-style meals and on the weekends when the dining area is expanded and thrown open to the public, it doesn't take long before the bookings fill the place. We can seat and feed around one hundred and fifty people plus the residents.

"Once every two months, the Bathurst Swingers Club book for dinner on a Saturday night. They usually number between 40 and 60. On that same night we get bookings from the golf club and the tennis club and the restaurant is soon fully booked.

"On this night, Andrea opens up the rest of the first floor, and in particular, the Pink Room. I would hazard a guess that nowhere in rural Australia is there a more appreciated event than what happens in the Pink room.

"As people finish dining, many, if not most, will gravitate towards the Pink Room where the floor is covered in mattresses and pillows. I'll let you find out for yourself what happens there.

"And by the way, this upcoming Saturday will see it all in action. I've already finished taking bookings, and I've even reserved you a seat, and if you do turn up, look out! I've sat you next to Tegan, our events manager and known to just a few of us as the queen of warm ups.

"The Pink Room is a bonus for our regular paying holidaying guests. It offers the only real opportunity for these women to interact with strangers, especially men. They love it!

"I should also mention that Dean and I joined the Sydney Swingers club a year ago and it was just what we needed.

Best of luck!

THREE

ON HER OWN

It was Mary's first day as the office manager. She was all alone and already missing Leanne. But she was soon absorbed in her work and only a polite cough from someone at the counter brought her to focus on the world around her.

A woman was smiling at her. She was well dressed and quite beautiful in a masculine sort of way.

"Hello. It's Mary isn't it? I'm Georgina from Number 4. I wanted to buy a dildo if possible. I forgot to pack mine. Can you show me what you have?"

Mary rose and came over to the counter, wearing a friendly smile.

"Hello Georgina. I certainly can."

Mary reached down and brought a tray from under the counter.

"There isn't a large range but I understand that the selection comes with managements recommendations. I take it you know what you are looking for?"

Georgina looked closely at the offering then raised her head and smilingly asked Mary if she could personally recommend any of the models sitting on display in their sealed cellophane wrappers.

Mary was caught unawares and felt herself beginning to blush and then, without thinking, pointed to the model she had enjoyed with Leanne, and heard herself speaking.

"Only that one there, Georgina, and I must say that I found it very satisfying."

Too late, Mary realised that she had fallen into a trap and now was fully exposed to the smiling Georgina.

Georgina lifted up the cellophane package and pretended to inspect it. Then she looked directly at Mary and smiled a loving smile that Mary could not ignore.

"I would love it if you would visit me tomorrow, Mary? I would so like to know you better. I have Judy from Unit 7 coming. She's already excited. We usually meet here each year.

"I think you will like Judy. She's in her mid-forties. She's quite overweight but that might be why she is such a lot of fun. Very touchy-feely! Like me, she also has a sexy secret which I'm sure you will love when you discover it."

Georgina gave a knowing smile and reached across and took Mary's hand in hers.

"I think you would enjoy our company, Mary, something different, maybe. Will you come at around two o'clock? Would you be happy to watch and play?" Then she picked up the dildo and proffered her credit card.

Mary smiled back, took the card and processed the purchase through the system, thinking as she did so that the invitation from this super attractive woman from Unit 4, sounded very exciting.

"I would love to visit you, Georgina and meet your fun friend. I'll be there just after two."

Wearing a tight black skirt and low-cut top and in her white garter belt and suspenders along with light blue stockings and strappy high heels and wearing her finest underwear, Mary found herself trembling with excitement when she rang the door bell of unit 4.

The more she thought about Georgina, the more she experienced that lovely but quite rare sensation in her vagina. She knew why she was getting damp between her legs.

Anticipation of the likely unexpected events of a sexual kind drove Mary's excitement to a new level, and she was to be immediately rewarded.

Mary was hardly inside the door of Unit 4 before an enthusiastic Georgina wearing only a garter belt and white stockings and high heels, grabbed and embraced her and pushed her up against the wall, covering Mary's face and neck with kisses.

Mary noted that Georgina had an allover tan and she looked like a woman who worked out. Her breasts where a modest size and shapely and when she dragged Mary's hands around to her buttocks, Mary discovered a well defined little bum.

The feelings and emotions that Mary felt were just fine.

Georgina immediately shoved a hand up Mary's skirt and felt between Mary 's legs and enthusiastically rubbed her crotch. Mary heard the woman moan and murmur in a little girl voice "yes, yes, beautiful, I want it," while she carried on kissing Mary's lips and enthusiastically fingering her wet panties.

Then Mary felt a hand unzipping her skirt which fell down around her ankles. She heard an excited squeal and realised that another person was taking an interest in her.

Georgina moved her mouth back for a moment, long enough to inform Mary that Judy was madly excited about Mary's arrival. "She's already totally naked but she wants us to stay in our underwear."

Mary felt caressing hands on her legs followed by licking and kissing on her thighs above her stocking tops and she realised that she really wanted to eyeball Judy.

"This is all part of her warm-up before she gets into her fantasies. She'll want both of us on our knees while she mounts us with a dildo. She will be giving it to us in true doggy fashion. She likes to imagine she's a dog and she might even make growling noises. Best just be whatever she wants you to be. It will be fun, I promise you."

Mary looked down and saw a very short fat naked woman fondling Georgina between her legs.

Judy looked up at Mary, proffering a beautiful smile on an angelic face.

With her short black hair and her bright lipsticked lips above huge breasts and a rotund belly, she was like a creature from a fairy tale. She had tiny hands and fingers and on the end of her plump legs were doll-like feet. Her finger and toe nails were bright red. She wore long black eyelashes over her big grey eyes which she slowly closed and opened provocatively. If she'd had pointy ears she could have been a cosplay pixie.

Under different circumstances and if she was fully clothed, Judy would be the most desirable doll figure to ever grace a little girls bedroom.

"I think she's ready for some attention and I know she will enjoy showing you her special secret. Okay, Jude! We're coming to get you."

The pixie figure giggled and rolled over onto her back on the carpet, lifting her legs and shaking them excitedly. Then she fixed her eyes on Mary, parted her legs wide and pointed a finger towards the location of her private parts. Suddenly, Mary was looking at Judy's secret.

"Oh my God! She's got a willy!"

It slowly dawned on Mary that this was not a giant clitoris. Instead of a vulva, what she was looking at was a tiny scrotum and with a tiny perfectly formed penis.

Mary felt Georgina's hands slide into the back of her knickers and cup her buttocks, and her body suddenly relaxed. Mary just wanted to belong to the two of them and their fantasies.

"She wants your mouth, Mary, and I want you on your knees. You will be my bitch while I fantasise being a randy dog. You can make us both happy and we'll do our best to make you happy."

Mary didn't need telling a second time. She slid to the floor as Georgina slid her pants down over her ankles. Out of the corner of her eye Mary saw Georgina lifting something out of her knickers and wondered what she was about to get. But in front of her now was something special.

Judy reached up and dragged Mary to her bosom and fastened her lips on Mary's and moments later their tongues danced a duet in their mouths. Mary felt the dolls legs wrapping around her waist and Judy pulled Mary into her, thrusting up at her with her abdomen and rubbing her little penis against Mary's belly.

Then she opened her legs wide and gently pushed Mary's head down towards her crotch, indicating that she wanted her to investigate her special loving secret.

Judy's appendage was stiff and Mary could have sworn that it smiled at her and waved and as she bent low and opened her mouth to savour it, something nice began happening to her own special parts as Georgina lubed her pussy and anus then arched her back and readied herself for her doggy impersonation.

Mary leant back and welcomed what she had assumed would be the feel of a dildo against her cunt. Instead, she felt a real cock and the truth suddenly dawned on her. Both women were transexuals; women with cocks. Not that it was in any way less sexy. It was simply unexpected.

It took only a few moments for Mary to assimilate this information. Suddenly she was enjoying the new experience and wallowing in the sensuous pleasure it provided.

Judy's beautiful little penis moved itself around Mary's mouth just like any little cock and the sensation was divine.

Mary recalled many years ago being with a man with a tiny penis. To her surprise they had a great sexual encounter and afterwards, she just couldn't stop sucking his little willie.

Then Georgina suddenly pushed into Mary in a rough and animal fashion and the pixie beneath her squealed with excitement, and in her little voice called out, "Fuck the randy bitch! Good boy! Yes, Yes, don't stop! I can feel it too!"

Mary had heaven in her mouth and heaven in her cunt and it was all she could do not to cum straight away. Then a reassuring voice from behind whispered, "You can come whenever you want, you beautiful bitch, but I should warn you, I won't be stopping."

The hard rapid strokes of the beautiful Georgina's hard cock along with the exciting movement in her mouth resulted in a gigantic orgasm for both Mary and for the plump little pixie spread below her who banged her little feet on Georgina's chest, screaming,

"Oh God! Thank you so much. I love you both to bits. Please don't stop."

The super Georgina was in full flight and for just s moment Mary imagined she was being fucked by a man although that didn't really matter. In fact she was now in love with the idea of having trans lovers.

Georgina uttered an unexpected girly squeal and bit into the back of Mary's neck. Then she pulled out her cock and within seconds rammed it back in only this time into Mary's bum. She was quite violent and Mary was thankful for the lubricant but once she had established a rhythm, they settled into a delicious anal orgy with the pixie moving about and licking and caressing every part of them.

Then Judy positioned her bum against Mary's face so that she was forced to lick her little pink hole. Then she bent down further so that Mary could explore her loose hanging scrotum, all the while gurgling and giggling and sighing and gasping and never ever silent.

"I'm coming, you bitch," gasped a frantic Georgina. She came with much screaming and they all joined in with a chorus of wailing and grunting and slapping each others bodies then collapsed onto the carpet.

"Georgina! You first, you beautiful slut bitch. On your knees."

"In a minute, darling, I need a moment."

Georgina and Mary where now locked in a loving display of mutual sloppy kissing. Then Georgina broke away and whispered, "Fuck my arse you beautiful woman and make me come."

Judy moved over to Mary and caressed her lips with the end of the dildo. "You will need this, you slutty bitch. Let me strap it on when your ready."

Mary rode Georgina's wonderful cock cowgirl while fondling the woman's breasts and staring down at her beatific face. Georgina's eyes were partly closed and her big red lips flopped open as she panted and moaned. With her other hand, or rather her fingers, Mary masturbated the tubby pixie's little cock, all the time thinking how sex couldn't get any better than this.

Mary spent the next half hour giving both ladies what they wanted, shagging their arses with the dildo and sucking their cocks. She finished them both off with blow jobs, unexpectedly coming with them as they screamed with excitement.

Georgina and Judy laid back and laughingly declared that the lovely Mary was now the queen of the trannies.

"Will you visit us again, Mary? You are a dream come true. Say you will give us this all over again, Mary. Please?"

Mary laughed and promised that she would make herself available again, just so long as they allowed her plenty of sucking time.

"Oh yes, we will for sure, won't we Judith?"

FOUR

LEANNE'S HOLIDAY

Mary's work mate, Leanne and her husband, Dean were back from holidays but Leanne wouldn't start back at The Pine's for nearly a fortnight.

"Yes, we had a wonderful time, Mary. We'd love you to come over on Sunday, if you would and we can tell you all about it. I've missed you."

"I've missed you too, Leanne. And thanks for nominating me to stand in for you with Tegan. Given you've been her tag partner in the past, you know exactly how exciting that would have been."

"Oh yes! I missed out badly there, didn't I? I trust you enjoyed yourselves?"

Mary assured her that a fantastic time was had by all.

The two laughed and said how they looked forward to seeing each other.

Over an enjoyable lunch, Leanne and Dean retold the highlights of their trip away.

Caravanning wasn't something that attracted Mary, or it wasn't until the couple mentioned the swingers night. Then it did get interesting.

We'd been told about it by a close friend of Ursula but wasn't really expecting anything much to happen. But then when we turned up quite late in the day at the special area allotted to the Sydney Swingers Club at the caravan park at Port Douglas, we had our hands full; literally.

There was a smorgasbord and barbecue in progress and modest amount of alcohol had been consumed.

We were immediately approached by an elegant woman named Caroline who welcomed us and invited us to join in whatever took our fancy.

We had stood looking around for only a few moments when a woman approached Dean and smiled seductively and put her hand on the front of his trousers and said her name was Lorraine and invited him to come and meet her mother and sister and look at their caravan.

At that moment I felt a hand on my backside and heard Caroline's voice.

"Oh, Bertie! Be patient. Leanne has only just got here."

Dean looked at me with a sheepish grin and suggested I chill out and take in the sights. I replied that those tits he was staring at had been a good place for him to start and that in the meantime, I hoped I would be able to find something equally exciting that I could enjoy.

Then Dean disappeared into a nearby caravan with the woman with the outstanding tits and I didn't see him for hours.

Caroline and her Bertie insisted I inspect their caravan and once I was inside, the excited couple proceeded to take advantage of my apparent abandonment.

Caroline was the first to make a move. She took me by the hand and led me to their double bed. Then she pushed me down and began to unbutton my top and then kiss my breasts while at the same time pushing her hand up under my dress and palming my already moist pussy.

As she was doing this I looked up and saw Bertie brandishing his formidable cock.

Caroline looked up also, then she asked me if I did anal?

"It's Bertie's favourite and he is very good at it. I sometimes give him my bum and let him do it to me for ages while I watch my favourite soap on television. And I give him a good sucking during the ads. We both so enjoy it. He's got such a lovely cock, darling."

What the lovely lady said excited me and I very quickly fell into sync with my seducers and murmured that I did enjoy anal and that I would welcome her husbands attention to my bottom at the appropriate time. Caroline turned to her husband and told him that he could have my bottom as soon as she had finished with me.

It was all becoming most enjoyable or I should say, extremely exciting.

Then three friends of Bertie's arrived back from fishing and saw that they might be in the right place at the right time and decided to join in.

Caroline smiled at the three in that special way women can and complained to the three that she hadn't had a cock all day.

The men obligingly pushed her down onto her back on the bed and Caroline quickly removed her knickers and demanded that all three must show her their cocks and then shag her and then make a substantial offering between her lips before heading home to their wives.

As the men dutifully shed their trousers and did Caroline's bidding, Bertie came over and took my hand, lifted me off the bed and led me to a little alcove along the passageway.

"Now, dear lady, I have some lube here. Will we do it standing up? We could start with you bending over and then change to have you in a kneeling position on that settee there."

While I removed my knickers, I informed him that I would like to have a suck of him before we did any of that and he obligingly waved his upright cock in my direction.

Bertie's cock was quite a mouthful and I was excited at the prospect of feeling him sliding it into my bum.

When I stopped sucking and turned and bent over, Bertie lubed me and then gave it to my like I wanted it, hard and fast.

"Oh yes, you bastard, I love it! Keep giving it to me and don't stop. Yes! Keep going and don't stop, please don't stop."

After such a lengthy session of exquisite bum bashing and

Bertie's ejaculation, I staggered back out to the double bed to look for Caroline. She was just sucking off another man who had unexpectedly arrived looking for Bertie. The other three had disappeared and it was only moments later the fellow roared and slumped forward and Caroline was grinning at me while gulping down her final offering.

"Oh God, they were all so good. I always think that if you can be the first to get a man into your mouth quite early in the morning, they will cum so much better; just my observation over many years, darling."

As the last man left, accompanied by Bertie who was telling him about something they should see up at the Swingers festival, Caroline pulled me onto the bed. She rolled me onto my tummy and proceeded to lick her husband's cum trickling from my bum.

Then we relaxed with kissing and licking and lots of laughter as this amazing woman recounted some of her sexual exploits.

Mary was feeling incredibly randy at this point and took hold of Leanne 's hand.

"You had better stop now darling or I swear I'll head off to Port Douglas and look for the swingers."

Dean who was usually quite silent, added a final word.

"My darling wife and I enjoyed ourselves very much and we have a booking to repeat the holiday next year. You might like to join us, Leanne. I know I'd enjoy your company."

Leanne laughed, interpreting her husbands thoughts into erotic foreplay.

"As it happens darling, you won't need to wait until next year as far as Mary is concerned. One of the reasons I invited her over today, was so that she could experience and enjoy our wonderful Pedro.

"We will need to borrow your cock for that, darling. Will you willingly submit to providing my beautiful girlfriend with a chance to be your cow-girl? I will be there with you both, of course. And I will introduce Pedro to Mary's bum."

Mary felt herself blushing at her friends forthright request to her husband.

"Dean might not be up for it, Leanne. I doubt he'll find me as exciting as his wife. I don't want to embarrass him or put him under pressure. You don't need to prove your story about Pedro. I believe you, darling."

"Just get yourself up on the bed, darling. We'll do the rest."

Mary surrendered to Leanne 's magic fingers and Dean's soothing bottom rubbing and very soon she found herself minus her knickers and on top of the lovely man and riding his superb cock. Leanne had stripped to just her undies and was obviously enjoying giving Mary to her husband as a present he hadn't expected.

Mary closed her eyes and moved up and down, relishing the feeling of Dean's beautiful solid member in her vagina.

Then she felt Leanne's fingers wiping lubricant on and in her anus.

"Are you ready, darling?" whispered an excited Leanne. "Just say stop if you find it uncomfortable, and I'll take Pedro away."

Mary felt very languid and answered slowly.

"Your husband's cock is wonderful, Leanne. I don't know if I need anything more. But yes, I'm ready for my surprise."

Leanne busied herself with a tube of lube on Mary's anus and then she reached down to where they kept Pedro under the bed and in a mummy sort of voice said, "Now mummy's got a special friend she wants you to meet and she wants you to be nice to her, just like you are to mummy."

Mary felt something fluffy nestling in between her buttocks. Then she felt Leanne putting the soft toy's hidden rubber dildo up close to Mary's bum and moving it around. She also felt Leanne breathing heavily on her neck and then the woman's lips kissing her and nibbling her ear. Then she felt Leanne holding Pedro down firmly on Mary's backside and she heard her whisper to her husband. "Ready, darling."

Suddenly, Mary screamed.

"Oh my God! Oh my God! Stop! No! Don't stop! Oh yes! Keep doing it, Oh! Don't stop! Oh my God!"

Leanne screamed too. She had experienced it often but had never actually watched it happen. Seeing their mechanical pet thrusting on top of her girlfriends rear end was so exciting and her free hand flew between her legs so that she could rub herself.

Mary couldn't stop herself putting her hand around and feeling Pedro's magic rubber dick.

"Oh Leanne! This is so beautiful. I could never have imagined it being so good."

It wasn't just Pedro who was putting in the effort. Dean had responded to Leanne's increased vigour and was pounding her vagina with added gusto.

Mary screamed and came and Leanne screamed and came and Dean yelled and came and then Dean did something clever on his smartphone and Pedro gave a final heave inside Mary's ravaged and totally excited anus.

"What a good boy you are. I could see that Mary really enjoyed that. Thank you, Dean. You're getting to be a wiz with Pedro."

Leanne gently lifted Pedro and placed him back under the bed. Then Leanne just could not resist sliding a leg over her friends delicious rear end and humping her. Mary welcomed her quietly by pushing back up towards her while making sure she didn't dislodge Dean from her now saturated and slippery pussy.

Dean kissed Mary and thanked her for such a lovely fuck and Mary thanked him back. Then Leanne, not to be left out, thanked them all, including Pedro, for a stunning performance.

———

As Mary headed for the front door, Leanne and Dean accompanied her to say farewell.

"The offer stands for the holiday next year if you can make it, Mary."

Mary thanked them for such a wonderful day and their kind

holiday offer. She thanked Dean especially for making himself available. Leanne looked at Dean then at Mary.

"We don't have to wait that long, my dearest loves. Dean could surely manage a repeat performance before then, could you not, darling?"

Mary looked lovingly at the two of them and smiled and Dean answered his wife.

"I'll be guided by you and our new toy Pedro, of course. Whenever it's okay with them it will be okay with me."

Everyone laughed.

"If that is the case, then Mary better just move in with us. We could be up for it every day. Of course I might want the two of them all to myself sometimes."

As Leanne walked Mary to the front gate, Mary said that there was something she always wanted to mention to Leanne but kept forgetting.

"I thought about it again after the warm-up night with Tegan and realised that there are a whole lot of interesting moments in our lives that we haven't talked about, Leanne."

"What, in particular, would that be, darling?"

"It might be fun to tell each other about our first experience with multiple cocks. What do you think? We might enjoy that."

Mary stood back and looked at her friend.

"What a great idea, darling; I'm excited about it already. And now I've got a lovely tingling feeling going up and down my spine remembering that first-ever time.

"Reliving those magic moments with my horny friend would be super sexy. Yes, lets get together soon and do it."

FIVE

QUEEN OF WARM-UPS

Mary had met Tegan on a few occasions when she came to the office to get details about staff records or commercial addresses to assist with event planning and such like.

Tegan was alway modestly dressed and very polite and Mary considered her most likely in a long term relationship and leading a conventional life. So it was a surprise when Leanne called Tegan the queen of warm-ups and that Mary would be seated next to her at dinner.

As the meal progressed and drinks were being happily consumed, a very different person emerged and Mary found it necessary to rethink the Tegan persona.

Mary noticed that Tegan had a special smile that she had never seen until now. It was both enticing and to the men sitting at the table, it was obviously provocative.

What Mary was about to discover would come as a shock. As the evening progressed, Tegan revealed her real self. Mary finally accepted that this plain looking woman could be transformed into a sex hungry creature capable of amazing planning skills when it came to organising men to do her bidding.

If Tegan's job label was Event Planner, she was certainly qualified to plan an orgy for herself and for her new friend, Mary. And before Mary had time to think things through, a voice announced the plan.

"I've been told you are someone who would enjoy a lot of cocks, Mary. Just read this before I text it to all the men."

Mary gave Tegan a friendly smile and commented that she had been known to entertain more than one man at a time. Then she read the message on Tegan's phone.

Warm-up in Room 17 next to the Pink Room. Two horny and willing Cum Queens wanting to fuck or suck. Back or front. FREE. 9 pm till 10 pm. See you there!

The message finished with a suggestive photo.

Mary read the message then looked at Tegan.

"Are you serious,Tegan? Is this allowed? And where did you get that photo?"

Tegan looked at Mary and then down at Mary below the edge of the table. Mary looked down and gasped. Unbeknown to her, Tegan, had put her hand on Mary's thigh and lifted her skirt and taken the picture.

Tegan smiled and her eyes flashed.

"A great pic Mary, and yes, it's worked for the past two years, darling. Are you up for it?"

Mary was thinking fast. The idea excited her but sending this message seemed so brazen.

"Who were you with last year, Tegan. Did you have a willing partner then?"

"Of course I did. Leanne has been my partner the past two times and would have been with me tonight except she's gone on holidays as you know. She recommended you."

Hearing that her favourite office manager had been a party to the event was reason enough for Mary to answer in the affirmative.

"Send the message, Tegan."

It didn't take long for the two woman to make themselves comfortable on the two semi raised old-style hospital beds in room seventeen. They removed their tops and skirts and displayed themselves to each other, all the time touching each other and giggling.

"You must tell me one day how you came up with this idea, Tegan. I'm intrigued. And I must confess I wouldn't have picked you as a player. You are the ultimate 'dark horse', darling."

"The psychologists all say I have a condition, the name of which I cannot pronounce. It only gets triggered when I'm in a crowd of males or confronted with sexual activities. I've twice experienced it with women, once at a Tupperware party and the other at a lingerie party.

"On the second occasion it ended up very interesting. Until then, I had no idea that most women were up for it given half a chance. And they were so inventive!

"The women were not in any hurry to leave the party. Suddenly the Tupperware disappeared into plastic boxes and sex toys appeared and were being handed around amid raucous laughter and excited shouting. I soon discovered that some of them were already in sexual relationships with each other, some of which had been going for years.

"Husbands had no idea that his Belinda from number 19 regularly called around to see his golfing mates wife, Anne at number 27. With the latest dildos purchased from the serenely innocent looking Tupperware lady and fitted inside moist vaginas and held in by their newly acquired sexy lingerie, they enjoyed much more than cake and coffee.

"Now, here is your mask, Mary. Keep it on so that you won't be recognised later. You know how it can be; you're just loading you're shopping cart at the supermarket or filling the car with petrol and there is a stranger grinning at you and he whispers "remember me?"

"It could be embarrassing."

The face mask was attractive and fitted comfortably.

Tegan produced a large tube of lubricant and squeezed some onto her fingers and applied it between her buttocks. Then she passed the tube to Mary who did the same. Then she walked over and unlocked the door.

"Are we all set then, Mary? One minute to go! Have fun!"

The two women laid on their stomachs in preparation for raising themselves up on their knees and displaying their womanly offerings. Tegan reached her hand across and took hold of Mary's hand and squeezed it and giggled.

It crossed Mary's mind that Tegan became a different person once she surrendered to her condition. She suddenly seemed more human and more humble and giving, and someone you could talk to quite easily.

Then they heard the door open. A group of surprised men laughed and called out as they looked appreciatively at the two beautiful naked backsides atop kneeling stockinged legs and heeled shoes.

Mary heard Tegan call out as the first cock made an entrance.

"Oh yes! Give it to me, please. I want all of it. Yes! Beautiful! More please."

Moments later, Mary just wanted to fade away in her excitement when she felt the first smooth head of a giant cock rubbing gently between her pre-lubed labia.

"Oh yes, you lovely man! Oh yes! That is what I want. You darling man. Let me have it!"

One cock followed another. Both women were beside themselves with sexual excitement and pure delight and neither was disappointed by any cock offered them, large or small.

The two women were kept busy for the full hour. As one man left, another took his place. Most time's the women were on their knees. Occasionally a man would mutter "on your back sweetheart" and have his way in the missionary position.

Mary soon relaxed into her slutty sex-loving role and she savoured each cock as it rubbed and shoved at her welcoming cunt, sometimes reaching down and squeezing and playing with a lucky man's equipment.

The men were generous and good humoured and there was banter between them.

"Oh, God! This cunt feels so beautiful. How's yours, Harry?"

"Fantastic, James. Better even than the two big girls at the office who gives it out each night after work, standing up against the wall in the stationery store room; and they're bloody terrific."

Mary couldn't imagine life without sex, be it with a man or a woman. She could have happily spent her waking hours sucking, licking and shagging a never ending line of men and letting them do whatever they wanted with her.

Mary never felt unsafe and if something happened she did not like, she would gently move things along. Her experiences with the opposite sex had always been positive.

As the crowd of men got bigger so the queue began to spread out around the two women. The men didn't want to stand in line. Suddenly cocks were being waved at them at both ends and Tegan and Mary found themselves in what could only best be described as a gentlemanly gang-bang.

Tegan looked across at Mary and called out.

"I think we're in for a storm, Mary. Hope you're okay with it?" to which Mary replied, "I just love this kind of weather, Tegan."

Both women soon found they had a cock in each hand, one or even two cocks standing in front of their mouths, and one in their cunt and with more waiting to get in. Then Mary felt a cock in her rear, excitedly rubbing against the other through the thin lining separating the cocks in her cunt and her bum and she thought how this was truly cock heaven

It was all systems go in the warm-up room.

Mary didn't think about much else at moments like this. The sheer ecstasy of being in this most vulnerable position and wanted by one man after another, filled her with happiness. And when the occasional slippery cock managed to give her a little orgasm, Mary smiled to herself and gave thanks to that day she and her friend Amber enjoyed their first multiple cocks at Ingrid's soiree all those years ago.

When all the men had left the room, Mary and Tegan rested and then Tegan got up and came over to Mary and gently laid on top of her and kissed her.

"That was so good, Mary. I hope you liked it too."

"Very much, Tegan. Couldn't have been better. Pity we can't get that every week. I think it would be good for me. I might even loose a bit of weight."

As the two laughed, Tegan's mobile made a sound indicating an incoming message.

Tegan read it and went quiet.

"Is everything okay, Tegan?"

"I think so darling but I need your opinion."

Tegan passed the phone to Mary.

2 horny-bitch residents want to clean up your pussies. Loving sucking and licking guaranteed. Text back 'Yes' if you want it.

"Well that sounds interesting, Tegan. I know a bit about our unusual residents. Enough to know that they would be turned on by the thought of getting a lot of what our happy men just left behind. Remember that they mostly have pets with whom they are very affectionate, putting things as delicately as possible. Licking up after each other is an activity they really enjoy.

"Will we try something different, my love? Or have you had enough for one day."

Tegan looked at Mary, excited by what she had said. She knew little about The Pines residents except that they were a little kinky when it came to their pets.

"I'm up for it but only if you want too, Mary."

Mary grinned.

"It might give new meaning to being finished off, darling. Lets say yes."

Tegan texted back:

Yes. Lock the door once you are in.

There was a tap on the door and Tegan called out for the visitors to come in.

Two women entered and stood staring at the reclining Mary and Tegan who were laying backs with their cum-flecked stockinged legs apart and their knees bent.

"Welcome! Help yourselves ladies. We've enjoyed at least a dozen or more cream pies each and even though a lot of what they gave us has already dribbled away, we are sure you will find enough.

"I'm Tegan and this is Mary. Do you know any of these ladies, Mary?"

"I certainly do, Tegan. They are regular guests here and I do know they are a very likeable bunch.

"Tegan and I are just resting so please make yourself at home and do whatever takes your fancy.

"We're both in that happy afterglow so I'm sure we'll both enjoy whatever you want to do with us.

A short and very plump woman in a tight mini skirt and probably in her late thirties, stepped forward and dropped to her knees in front of Tegan. Mary knew her as Ruth and she was with her friend, an extremely skinny long-legged younger woman known simply as Dot. Mary admired Ruth's fat but near perfect bare bum before turning to admire the skinny but interesting form of her friend.

Ruth introduced herself to Tegan then took no time in starting her sucking and slurping of all that was on offer between Tegan's legs, pausing every few seconds to swallow what she'd collected.

Mary looked at the younger Dot whose wide open eyes foretold her excitement. Mary smiled at her thinking how sexy the girl looked.

"I would love to feel your lips and tongue on my pussy, Dot. Please help yourself," Mary whispered.

The stick-figure woman walked slowly over on her stylish heels and moved up close to Mary. Mary smiled and took Dot's hand and put the young woman's long fingers on Mary's soaking wet hairy pussy and pressed them gently agains her clitoris.

"There, darling. I promise it won't bite. Lick me you gorgeous thing. I want to feel your tongue."

Dot responded, relaxing in Mary's kindness. She was soon lapping up the spoils of lust, her eyes closed and moans of excited satisfaction coming from deep down in her throat. When she stopped to swallow, she would gasp and look up longingly at Mary's lovely smile and more than adequate body, then plunge her face back into the perfumed forest for more.

Mary closed her eyes and panted softly as Dot's soft lips and tongue worked it's wonders.

Mary became aware that Ruth was talking to Tegan and very quickly and in response to the woman's request, Tegan rolled over and mounted the chubby kneeling woman's fantastic rear end. Then she humped Ruth's significant rear end, uttering slutty coarse messages in her ear while reaching around to rub the woman's excited and surprisingly large clitoris.

Dot stopped her slurping and looked at the two lying beside them.

"Oh Mary that looks so good, doesn't it?" Then Dot looked at Mary longingly.

"All right. You want to be my doggy bitch. I know. Say how much you want it, you beanstalk slut."

Dot looked at Mary in anticipation.

"I really want you to hump me Mary. Please?"

Mary swung herself up and pulled Dot's pants down around her ankles, staring at her amazing thin legs. Then she swung herself over her tiny backside. She had never ridden a bum so small. One hand could cover a butt cheek and the woman's pussy was tiny Mary discovered when she put a hand around and touched her.

The woman gurgled with excitement and whispered "Yes please, Mary. Oh, yes! Please do this to me for ever."

To Mary's great surprise, she discovered that Dot's bottom cheeks could clasp and squeeze Mary's sizeable clitoris, and when she moved backwards and forwards, the darling woman clamped her cheeks tighter to also enjoy the feeling.

"Oh my God, you crazy gorgeous creature. You feel fucking wonderful. Keep squeezing my clit between your butt cheeks, you scrawny slut. I'm going to come soon."

The two fell back and lay still, holding hands and breathing deeply.

Both had come at around the same time. Mary hadn't ever previously experienced what they had just done.

The shy woman panted, then she whispered in Mary's ear. "I would love you to do that again whenever you feel like it Mary. I so loved it. I'm here for another two weeks. Text me, please. I'll come and be your sex slave whenever you want me."

Mary smiled and whispered back, "I will definitely do that,

Beside them, Ruth was now on her back and Tegan was energetically fisting her.

"You have the slipperiest vagina in the world, you little slut. Now come for me you randy bitch! I can't reach in any further."

And come she did, with screams and the heaving mass of Ruth's oversized body threatening to flatten everyone around.

Four happy women smiled at each other, satisfied and in love with each other.

"I think these two sluts should go to the top of our slut list, Mary. We will want them again."

Ruth and Dot smiled happily at their two happiness providers.

"And we'll put them on top of our slut lovers list won't we, Dot?"

The four had a final hug before leaving.

Dot whispered in Mary's ear. "Can I text you my home address in Paddington, Mary? I share a large terrace house with my identical twin sister and a couple of lodgers."

"My sister likes what I like. We enjoy sharing. They would all love you, I'm sure."

Mary replied enthusiastically. "Please send it Dot. I would like that very much."

SIX

LEANNE'S CONFESSION

Leanne called Mary and asked if they could get together for that reminiscing moment they had spoken of on the phone earlier in the month. They had mentioned in their conversation that they should tell each other about their first experiences with multiple cocks.

Mary replied yes and invited her friend over on the following Monday, it being her day off.

"So! The question is, who will go first, darling?"

Mary laughed and said how it was going to be hard to decide.

"Given that we are close to the same age, maybe it should be the one that started the youngest. What do you think, Leanne ?"

"Well, it began when I was twenty-two. What about you?"

"Great! You start. I began at twenty-three."

Leanne grumbled about being first but then settled down to tell her tale.

I had gone to stay on a sheep and cattle property with mum's sister Jane and her second husband, George, and my step-brothers; his three sons, the twins, Clifford and James, and their older brother, Alfred. The boys were all a couple of years younger than me.

Jane and George had gone to Sydney for four days and would be staying with my parents. Because I was the eldest, I was designated the person in charge for the next two nights

I was not in a happy frame of mind having just broken up with my boyfriend. I wasn't missing him but I was missing our regular sex activities, Brad's only good point.

The only other person around the homestead was Beryl, the attractive forty-something cook and house keeper who lived in a little cottage at the back of the house and halfway to the shearing sheds. Beryl was always cheerful and I felt guilty being a bit moody around her.

"You'll get over it, Leanne. We all do."

Beryl advised me gently while staring at me with interest. She alway looked good and dressed stylishly despite her housekeeper activities.

"You need to find something or someone else, and quickly. You're not getting any younger."

Beryl laughed at her own silly joke.

I said goodnight to Beryl and then went and said goodnight to the brothers. They all smiled friendly smiles and wished me goodnight and sweet dreams.

I managed to get to sleep quite quickly, despite my moodiness. But a couple of hours or a bit less, later, I awoke thinking I had heard a scream. I lay still and listened. Then I heard the faintest of sounds coming from the direction of the shearing shed.

I rose and slipped on a night dress and sneakers and headed out the door, cautiously closing it to avoid waking up the boys.

As I came around close to Beryl's house, I realised that the sounds were coming from her place. It wasn't exactly party sounds. There wasn't any music, just Beryl's smooth deep motherly voice.

"Okay, boys! Who's next."

I was intrigued to say the least. And who belonged to the utility vehicles parked out front?

I spotted a gap in the curtains in the front window and cautiously peered in. I couldn't believe what I was seeing.

Three naked muscular and tattooed young men were taking turns fucking Beryl and everyone was having a good time; most of all, Beryl.

Beryl was laying back on the sofa totally naked and with a cock in each hand, with the third man thrusting between her legs.

My first impulse was to run in the front door and strip off my clothes and join them. But I stopped and thought about it and decided I should organise my own affairs and not poach cocks from somebody else.

I returned to my bed and masturbated to the vision of what I had seen. This made me feel a lot better and I felt I could now face life differently.

The next morning I woke up late. My stepbrothers had already headed out on horses to muster stock and wouldn't return until later in the day.

I wandered to the kitchen where Beryl was sitting at the kitchen table busy shelling peas. It seemed as though it was just another day for her. There was no indication of her activities of the night before.

Seeing Beryl's solid shapely legs caused a momentary upheaval in my body as I wondered what she had worn last night before her eager young men had relieved her of her clothes. I walked over to her and stood up very close.

Beryl turned and looked at me, then before anything was said she stood up and put her arms around me and hugged me tight.

"I can see you are desperate for a little TLC, Leanne," she whispered. Will you let me give you some? I need some myself."

"I took a deep breath and a tiny voice issued from me."

"Oh yes, Beryl! I'm desperate for some of that. I would love you to help me."

Beryl took me by the hand and led me into a nearby tiny guest bedroom and turned and lifted my dress over my head and then she unzipped her skirt and stepped out of it. Her eyes shone and she whispered that she too was in need of something special.

What followed was a beautiful coming together of two horny women; one who needed it because she hadn't felt loving hands for so long, the other because she had experienced more male love than enough and now really needed a big dose of what only a girl could offer.

Beryl dragged my hand in between her legs as at the same time she began to finger my vagina. I groaned and begged her to kiss me. Our lips met and we passionately kissed and tongued each other

I had experienced girl play with Jennifer, one of my college mates when she came to my room one night after fighting with her boyfriend. It was our first experience of girl on girl kissing and it led on to fingering and pussy licking. We would have extended our mutual enjoyment except that her parents and the family suddenly moved away and we never caught up with each other again.

Beryl was something different. She knew the limits of the female body and she made love to me not like a man but as a woman who was having a man on her own terms.

I came and then she came and then I came again. Then she made me get up and straddle her buttocks and ride and hump her beautiful rear end. Then we threaded our thighs and scissored one another. It was all done slowly and it was sublime.

When we lay back, holding hands and feeling dozy, Beryl ventured to say that she was going away for two nights.

"It's my sisters birthday in Armidale. I'll stay over for two nights and won't be back until the afternoon of the third day."

Then Beryl rolled over and looked at me.

"Can I make a suggestion, Leanne ?"

"Certainly, Beryl. I hope its rude."

"Well it is actually. May I suggest that while I'm away, you fuck your stepbrothers senseless? They need it and you definitely need it. And before you say another word, they all have very nice cocks. I've tried them! That was the month before last. They have each approached me numerous times since but I send them on their way, saying I don't know what they are talking about."

I couldn't believe what I was hearing.

"Beryl! I, I ...! Oh never mind! Tell me more, you deliciously wicked woman."

"I had noticed some Lad magazines under mattresses in their rooms when I was cleaning. Your aunt and uncle where away for a few days. I realised that it would be very wrong of me but then I'm known for doing things I shouldn't.

"I realised that I had some underwear similar to the model in the picture on the most thumbed page, including a suspender belt and stockings and a pair of high heels along with a set of lacy underwear. It was difficult getting it all on as I last wore them ten years ago and my figure had change considerably.

"Needless to say, dressing up worked wonders and I had a wonderful night of sucking and fucking. The lads were beside themselves with excitement and I had to slow them down so that they could keep going to satisfy my deep sexual hunger.

"I won't say any more darling. You won't need any special effects, I'm sure, you being so young and attractive.

"My only advice is to be strong and decisive about what you want while being your cute self at the same time.

"You will drive them mad, I know. And if you make them wait for their orgasms, they will love you all the more plus you'll get a lot more of what you're looking for.

"Oh, and one more thing, I had my work cut out getting them all into the one room at the same time. I suggest you tell them that you want to play hide and seek or something. I'm sure they will obey your every request.

"Finally, darling, I want to lick and suck you right now. Can we do that?"

"Oh yes, you certainly can, wicked woman but I have just one proviso."

Beryl looked at me with her shining eyes. "What is that, darling?"

"Show me your sexy underwear before you leave, please, in case I want to wear it. It might just get me there, more quickly."

I was a little nervous as I walked down to the television room in Beryl's frilly bra and her high heels. Everything seemed a tiny bit big for me but strangely, they made me feel very sexy. Perhaps it was partly caused by me knowing that what I had on had already been used to successfully seduce my stepbrothers a few weeks before.

I had covered myself with a silky dressing gown tied at the waist which gave a modicum of modesty. But only a tiny bit. The heels were a bit of a giveaway.

The boys all looked up as I came in then they quickly swung their heads back and looked again.

"Thought I'd go into town tonight. There's nothing much going on here. I can tell that you lot aren't much into girls."

I won't go into detail about who got their hands on what part of me first. To tell the truth, that is a bit of a blur.

I think Alfred led the charge, coming to sit beside me and then pulling me to him and kissing me passionately.

"You look bloody gorgeous, Sis. I'm free tonight if you want some fun."

Clifford and James, not to be left out, came over and I felt hands climbing up the back of my legs inside my dressing gown.

"Well, this a surprise! I was beginning to think that you boys didn't like me. Maybe I won't need to go out after all."

It was when I had Clifford at my lips and James trying to find a way to get to my tits and when Alfred pulled my hand over onto his now exposed beautiful cock, I knew it was going to be a good night.

I sat back and surveyed my suitors. They seemed quite ravenous and eager to discover my body.

"If my darling steps take off their trousers, I'll take off my dressing gown. Do you like that idea?"

Three stiff cocks were suddenly on display and a girl couldn't help but shudder with excitement.

"Now, who's cock will I suck first?"

It was all a bit of a scramble at first but then I assured them that we had all night and that I wouldn't be going to look elsewhere if they all promised to give my poor lonely pussy a good and proper shafting. Needless to say, they all agreed.

It took a little while to settle them down and set a nice regular pace. As I sucked one and tugged on another, I invited the third one to slip his cock into where it would be most appreciated. There was hardly a moment when I didn't have a cock in my very wet cunt.

I told the boys that I didn't want them to come until I'd had enough and then I would suck each of them off.

They all had a turn of me laying on the sofa. Then I knelt on the carpet and they enjoyed me in doggy mode. Then I rolled over and stretched out and reached up and managed to get two beautiful hard cocks into my mouth while the third one happily pounded my pussy.

It was getting late and I knew we should all be getting to bed.

"Now who's first?"

I sucked off all three eager cocks and swallowed mouthfuls of their cum. I loved it and so did they. Then I informed them that it was time for bed.

Then I asked them if they would like to repeat the performance the next night to which they all replied with a resounding cheer.

"Showered and shaved and here at 8 pm. Okay?"

I awoke quite early, and went for a pee. Then, dressed only in my nightie, I stretched and wandered to the kitchen. Last nights enjoyable activities with my step brothers had given me an appetite and I busied myself, cutting bread and working the old toaster.

As I turned to reach for the fridge door to retrieve the butter, I felt hands on my waist and I turned to welcome whoever it was.

Alfred's smiling face greeted me.

"Good morning, sis. Got a moment?"

I looked down at the front of his pyjamas and immediately saw what he was offering. His big red cock was protruding from his nightwear and it seemed even bigger than when I held it last night. Then I saw my other two steps, standing behind him and staring at me, each in their pyjamas and both with huge erections and smiling like they'd just opened the ultimate Christmas present.

I stared at each rigid cock on offer and couldn't help but be impressed and moments later, properly excited at the thought of sex before breakfast.

"Well, boys. I think between the three of you, you will have enough jam to spread on a girls toast. I'm going back to bed shortly so you all had better give it to me while I'm still awake. And I'll need to taste you all first before I let you fuck my wet pussy."

I went down on my knees on the kitchen floor and suddenly I had three huge happy cocks jostling for position for a turn in my more than willing mouth. It was a wonderful way to start the day.

Then I stood up and lay back on the kitchen table with my legs hanging over the side. I pulled my nightie up around my neck and smiled lovingly at their excited faces.

"Who's first. And remember, you all have to come inside me so I've got something to remember you by all day and before I line you up again tonight for your supper."

Alfred was first, ramming me with his wide-awake cock. It was divine, especially when he yelled and shot his hot load deep inside me.

James followed and took only moments to pour his juices into my now hot and very wet pussy.

Finally, Cliff lovingly kissed my belly and smiled and fed me with enough of his beautiful cock to make me shudder and more than happy. As he came, he lifted me up off the table and pulled me towards him.

I lay still for a few moments, languidly enjoying all the sensations running around in me. Then I swung myself off the table and straightened my nightie.

"Make sure you all eat a hearty breakfast, boys. And don't forget I'll want a repeat of last night in the television room at 8 o'clock."

I wandered off to bed and played with myself, coming quickly, and getting very sticky fingers.

I had, for the second time in 24 hours enjoyed multiple cocks and deep down, I knew that I would still want to have more.

Late in the afternoon I rose and showered and then I painted my toe and finger nails a bright red, and when they were dry, I went and dressed in Beryl's sexy clothes and as I wandered around practicing walking in high heels, I decided that I would go shopping for sexy underwear and shoes once I returned home.

I would find out what dressing slutty was really like and I looked forward to going to the singles club with my girl friends and looking like a whore and fighting off the young exec's desperate to get me up against a wall. I wanted to be a femme fatale, a siren, a beacon to all cocks to come and worship me between my legs.

Meanwhile, I contemplated the night ahead. I would make my step brothers run their hands all over me and kiss my ankles while I watched their cocks twitch and grow ever bigger, ready for my attention.

Eight o'clock and I was already wet between the legs from earlier and from my anticipation of the night ahead. I wanted to draw the whole thing out and enjoy a slow fucking and sucking session so that I could extend the ecstasy I felt being had by the boys and touching them.

When I arrived in the lounge, I was shocked to see that there wasn't just my three steps sitting around but also three more young men, friends who the boys had invited home.

For a moment I was nonplussed and a little angry that they had invited others without consulting me. But then as I looked around at the newcomers, I was struck by their innocent similarity to my step brothers and I was soon harbouring thoughts of more cocks to enjoy.

My arrival caused the expected stir. I hadn't bothered with a dressing gown, just bare essentials. A suspender belt and stockings and a pair of high heels along with a set of lacy underwear seemed sufficient. Suddenly it was obvious that any planning on my part was pointless.

Again, Alfred led the charge with Clifford and James close behind. The three new boys stood up and watched excitedly unsure what to do.

Nothing could have stopped what happened. My best laid plans would never have worked. I was now totally at the mercy of six horny young men and I knew they would have me in whatever way they wanted.

First Alfred held me up from behind and instructed Clifford to remove my knickers. Once they were removed and my pussy was on display, Alfred told their three new friends, Tommy, Freddy and Peter to put their hands between my legs and feel my pussy. They took no time at all in complying with his wishes.

Then Alfred announced that their aunty would like it if all present would show her their cocks. I was certainly happy with that and moments later, six beautiful cocks stood waving and calling for my attention.

At this point I figured that I should take a hand in organising my own orgy.

"Thank you very much. Before we go any further, I have one request and once that is fulfilled, you will be free to have me as you will.

"I want you all to sit down on the sofa and chairs and let me move around and suck your cocks. This will make me very happy and dare I say, incredibly horny for when you are later free to have me they way I'm sure you all want.

"Now! To your seats gentlemen. This lady wants her moment with your cocks. Until I get to each of you, feel free to touch my legs or breasts, but please be gentle."

Over the next three hours I sucked and fucked six delightful young men and when I finished they gave a rousing cheer and all said they wanted me as their girl friend to which I answered, "No you don't, boys. You want me as your whore and you can rest assured that I'll always be up for that."

Mary grabbed Leanne and dragged her down onto the carpet and humped her.

"You crazy sexy bitch. My pussy is positively running with juices. How can I have a better story than that? Oh you are such a cock and pussy tease, Leanne.

The two happy women eventually settled back with tea and cup cakes as Mary prepared to tell her story of her first time with multiple cocks.

SEVEN

MARY'S CONFESSION

I was twenty four and working for large finance company as a secretary.

One lunch time, along with my long term friend and colleague and flatmate, Amber, we lined up at the canteen hatch to collect our meals.

Ingrid, the regular supervisor in the kitchen called out. "Hello you dear old things. How many years is it now that you've been together? Twenty or more?" Her joke about us as an old couple was telling and I smarted under the implications of her message about how she perceived us even though I knew she was joking.

"Now I think you should both come to our place on Saturday. Bob and I are having our monthly soiree and I'm sure you would enjoy yourselves.

"You will have to be ready for a bit of fun. Some say it's more like an orgy but I tell them that it's no such thing.

"What people get up to is their own business. We just supply the finger food and drinks."

"You should both come. It will be something different and if you don't like it you can just leave. Say you'll come, Mary and I'm sure Amber will want to be there with you, won't you Amber. Keeping an eye on each other could be important. Anything could happen."

I looked at Amber and grinned. "We should go. We've got nothing planned and it could be fun. What do you say?"

Amber smiled back and said she would be happy to give it a try.

Ingrid smiled lovingly at her. Then she indicated she wanted to whisper something to us and we leant forward.

"Make sure you wear a dress or a skirt, darlings. It helps a lot if you get a bit carried away and want to join in, so to speak."

I mumbled that we would and said we looked forward to seeing her there.

———————

We had fun dressing for our night out. Each critiqued the other's outfit. We had already agreed that tonight could be a resounding success with hot romantic results or it could be just plain boring like most parties.

"That dress is so slutty, darling. You will be arrested before we even get there," I called out to Amber from my bedroom as she glided past my door.

"Ingrid would approve, I'm sure."

"Okay then! I'll go for my shortest skirt. You can see suspenders and you can definitely see flesh above my stocking tops. So slut! We will be fighting the men off from the moment we walk through the door."

Amber laughed and commented. "Wishful thinking, you randy sexpot; and may the sluttiest woman win!"

The conversation between the two of us carried undertones of wishful thinking. We had both been experiencing a dearth of suitors in recent times and it was beginning to tell.

———————

There was already a lot of people at Ingrid and Bob's house when we got there.

Music was playing from somewhere out in the back garden. It was already dark and the shadows of the mood lighting the sounds of people moving about and laughing suggested that this was the place to be.

I followed Amber in through the front door and we slowly made our way along a crowded corridor. Half way along, I felt a hand on my backside and I turned only to find an attractive woman smiling at me.

"Nice butt, darling. Come back this way soon."

I smiled, but as I turned to keep moving, I noticed that another woman had her hand up my admirers skirt.

This could indeed be the place to be and in my head I replayed Ingrid's remarks about wearing a dress or skirt. Then I recalled how she had told us that it helps if you want to join in; and then the fun Amber and I had working out what to wear.

As I moved along the corridor behind Amber, I was super aware that people were just starting to discover each other and I felt a sudden thrill run through my body. I reached out in front of me and gently groped Amber's backside through her tight skirt and she turned and smiled.

"Well, that's a start Mary. Now lets hope someone we don't know gives my butt a try."

Amber and I looked into a number of rooms and witnessed the early stages of people getting together.

Two early moves seemed to be popular. Pressing someone against a wall was one and it seemed to be the prelude for much of what was about to be enjoyed by both parties.

A hand up someones skirt was equally in evidence. Occasionally I noticed a woman's hand exploring the front of a man's pants, usually brought about by his having his hand firmly in place somewhere under her skirt.

Amber took my hand, partly not to loose me and partly to signify our being a couple.

We had reached the end of the main passage and headed out into the garden area.

Across the lawn we spied a small cottage and sauntered over to it. It had probably been a granny flat. A man stood outside, smoking a cigarette and when we approached the front door, he moved in front of us and in a low voice said, "Sure you both want to?"

We smiled and Amber answered, "You make it sound scary. So that's even more reason to let us in?"

"You seem very young. I wouldn't have picked you."

The man smiled back and moved closer to the door, looking back at them and saying, "Guess you know what you want."

The man knocked five times on the door. We heard a bolt being slid aside and moments later, two arms shot out and we were dragged into the almost dark room.

There were people everywhere, mostly men. The floor seemed alive with bodies on mattresses.

Amber called out as she was dragged away but I didn't get a chance to find out what she was saying. I was immediately pinned to a wall and a man's hand took control between my legs.

I tried to speak but then I was being kissed by a woman which gave me a moment of comfort, but then fingers were pulling at my top and my breasts seem to just pop out, seemingly intent on being seen, Then they were being ravished by the mouth of a man with a stubble.

My mind ran through a short catalogue of possible responses. Warning bells began to ring. Then two things happened.

The woman reappeared and took hold of my arm and whispered that she was one of three Ladies Angels in the room. She said her name was Martha. She said that the Angels attended every month and were there to ensure that women were protected and hopefully got what they came for. She also mentioned that my friend was being watched over by another Ladies Angel and wasn't far away and was safely starting her adventure, just as I was.

I was starting to accept that I was safe and now I could explore what was going on here. Before I could plan what I would do next, Mr Stubble took hold of my hand and folded my fingers around his huge penis.

I wasn't expecting this and interestingly, I wasn't expecting to feel the excitement that ran through me as the man's huge lump of meat stretched itself and pulsated with excitement simply from feeling me holding it.

I felt suddenly powerful and, dare I say, hungry for more.

Then, without me letting go of him, Mr Stubble led me further into the room and pulled me down on to a mattress and I found myself on my back amongst other men and women, all of whom seemed to be enjoying each other.

I was still holding onto Mr Stubbles cock. He seemed to be smiling down at me in the dull light, then he reached back and put a hand around each of my ankles and lifted my legs up and apart. The he removed my hand from his cock and immediately I felt myself opening my pussy to receive his giant offering.

Suddenly I was filled like I never had been before. I had totally engulfed Mr Stubble's huge penis and my erstwhile sexual hunger was being satisfied at last.

I was still vaguely attempting to make an intellectual assessment of my situation despite my overwhelming bodily desire to simply go with the flow. Then I heard a familiar voice speaking to me and I quickly turned my head to look at the speaker.

There was a beautiful vision lying beside me. Ingrid lay back with her legs up and knee's bent and with her stockinged feet performing pirouettes and occasionally rubbing the thighs of the man on top of her.

"So glad you could make it, Mary. Amber is here on my other side and she seems very happy with what she's getting."

As Ingrid spoke, she interspersed her words with gasps and eye rolling and murmuring words of encouragement to the muscular tattooed man who was leisurely shafting her.

"I get this every month. I love it! And it keeps me going for weeks."

I noticed movement behind Ingrid and looked and saw another man with his cock in his hand, awaiting his turn at the lovely lady. Ingrid looked so at home with what she was having and many questions bubbled up but I was too busy to ask.

Then I looked over the head of the man pleasuring me and saw two heads seemingly lined up behind him, both straining to look at me in my semi naked pleasuring situation. I was a little apprehensive but also excited.

"I've been on my back for an hour or more now and I think Tim is my fifth for the day. I should get up and stretch and maybe go over and put myself onto the Slut Table behind us. It's more rough and tumble, but one can move around a bit and it offers lots of cocks to fuck and suck."

"Oops! Here I come again. He is so good. That is my third with him."

Ingrid arched her back and yelled and then she shook all over, dislodging the source of her pleasure. Then she moved and closed her legs and thanked the man.

"Hope I'll find you here again next month, Tim. I really enjoyed that."

When Ingrid left I looked across at Amber and she looked over at me and we both grinned.

She was about to welcome a new man between her legs, the second for the day, she told me later. She smiled up at him and called out that she was moving over towards me and that he should follow her.

Soon we were lying side by side and holding hands. Mr Stubble had given me up and a Mr Hairy Chest was waving his tool in front of my crotch. Feeling happy to have my friend safely by my side made me more relaxed and I looked up at my new suitor and found myself smiling at him.

"Be my guest." I found myself saying quite loudly and with a welcoming smile.

Suddenly I was being energetically taken by a second meaty cock and was shocked to suddenly find myself orgasming just moments later. Amber felt it and squeezed my hand and just as quickly she threw herself upwards and came in response to her second man pushing into her.

We both strained our necks to reach across to reach each others mouths and we kissed and tongued each other, something we had never thought of doing before. Then both our bodies shook again, likely caused by a combination of the excitement of our sudden discovery of hot kissing along with the wonderful feeling of the two new cocks.

Then Amber and I laid back with our legs up and bent. We relaxed into our private heavenly place of a soft wet cunt being pleasured by hard and active cocks.

This was what Ingrid said she lived for. Suddenly and with a sort of mutual understanding, Amber and I began a new phase of our life, one which allowed a full expression of our sexual selves.

From that moment on, multiple cocks would be something we both looked for and sometimes even shared. And from that day on, we both made sure we never missed a soiree at Ingrid and Bobs ever again. Oh yes! And Amber and I found we could relive moments simply by cuddling up and describing our soiree adventures and kissing and fingering and licking each other at home and enjoying wonderful orgasms together. Now that is friendship at its best.

EIGHT
THREE'S A CROWD

I was going out with a young man my age named Jeremy. We weren't doing much romantically. He would kiss me goodnight at my front gate and we did occasionally get almost passionate in his tiny Fiat 500 when he dropped me home.

There was a moment when, in the darkened picture theatre while watching a James Bond movie, he put his hand up my skirt and fingered me through my knickers. I responded by undoing his jeans and getting my hand in to feel his stiff cock through his underpants, but that only happened once.

Things didn't look at all promising in the sex department and I began to realise that Jeremy was too young for me. Something held him back and I figured I needed someone with more experience.

We were both at university and most days would visit the canteen together, we seemed like an old married couple.

The university's head janitor, Dave, was a lot of fun and he and I had an ongoing risqué dialog to do with his broom stick. The door of his janitor quarters bore the sign 'Broom Cupboard' and we would always laugh about him wanting me to come inside to see his broom sticks.

Dave's wife, Jenny, was a fun loving sexy woman who worked in the kitchen of the university dinning room. Like her husband, she was always up for a joke, usually a rude one and I really liked both of them despite Dave's ongoing threat to show me his broomstick.

Jeremy's birthday was happening in a few days and he and Lisa were both looking forward to it.

When Lisa mentioned the upcoming birthday to Jenny and also confided in her that things could be better in the sex department, the fun-loving lady suggested that Lisa could perhaps give Jeremy something special and sexy at the party, alternatively, she could flirt with other men and watch to see how he reacted.

"The party might get him going a bit, especially if he takes a drink. It's worth a try."

It was party night and a large number of Jeremy's male friends were in attendance, some with girlfriends and sisters or cousins, and there were a few women on their own.

Lisa found herself chatting to an attractive woman named Rosa who appeared to be around her own age and who nonchalantly informed Lisa that she was Jeremy's previous girlfriend.

After the initial shock, Lisa took advantage of the situation and cautiously inquired from Rosa the reason the two broke up.

"Oh, we got on just fine, Lisa. But I found myself feeling a bit inadequate and decided to move on. I could never excite him. It was only a little bit later that I found out from one of Jeremy friends–Big Mac, standing against the wall over there–that I was in fact, the third party in our relationship."

Lisa couldn't believe what she was hearing; another woman?

Lisa found herself commiserating with her new friend and saying that she was feeling unhappy in the relationship too.

"What happened? Who was she? What did you do?" The questions came quickly and Lisa wanted answers.

Rosa looked at Lisa apologetically.

"Maybe you don't really want to know. I shouldn't have mentioned it. Sorry!"

Lisa assured her that she did want to know.

"I'm thinking of breaking it off, anyway. So tell me Rosa, who was he seeing?"

Rosa looked at Lisa's face and understood where she was coming from. She'd been there herself.

"Well, the woman is much older than Jeremy. She was a friend of his late mother who suffered bouts of severe depression.

"Her name is Camila, and from when Jeremy was in his teens, he lived with Camila when his mother was taken into care, which was sometimes for months at a time.

"One can only speculate as to what and how things happened between him and his mum's friend.

"I first set eyes on her at last years birthday party which makes me wonder if she might appear today. Maybe this will be a turning point for you, Lisa, just as it was for me a year ago.

"She doesn't seem to be here at the moment, but keep an eye on Jeremy. Last year she simply came through the door and quickly led him away."

Lisa was not quite dumbfounded, probably more intrigued. She quickly ran through Jeremy and her recent activities together, realising that nothing had happened and in fact her emotions simply felt permanently on hold.

"Well, I'm so glad you've told me, Rosa. I suppose I haven't left him because I felt sorry for him. Now I don't need to feel that way any more. Thank God!"

Lisa glanced across the room at Jeremy and then gasped. "She's here Rosa. Is that her?" Rosa turned her head to look.

"That's her all right! Count to twenty slowly and I bet they will have left the room.

Lisa didn't get to twenty before the overtly sexualised older woman in a miniskirt and heavy stockinged legs and wobbling on her high heels, took Jeremy's hand and led him out the far door.

"Oh my God! So that is the reason he kept it in his trousers when he was with me."

Rosa laughed.

"And his hands to himself."

A tall man suddenly appeared beside them. Big Mac had also watched what had happened to his mate.

"I could see the Rosa was bringing you up to date, Lisa? I'm sorry I wasn't in a position to say anything. A bloke grassing on his friend can only look like he's trying to move in on his girlfriend. A blokes thing, I know, but I'm sure you'll understand."

Lisa and Rosa laughed and thanked Big Mac for his words of wisdom. Then Rosa gave Big M a cheeky smile.

"So is it okay to chat up his ex-girlfriends now, Mac? Surely there comes a time when you feel sorry for the poor things and want to offer them comfort. Who knows? Surely this could be just the right time?"

Lisa loved what her new friend had said and watched as the handsome man blushed.

"A fair comment, Rosa. It's a bit early in the night for me to consider such things but I hope neither of you are leaving just yet. And you wouldn't want to miss the floor show. Jeremy's Camila will be out when she's finished with Jeremy and you'd better be ready for that."

The two lovely ladies linked their arms in a show of teasing and camaraderie, then looked at each other then stared back at Mac.

"What do you mean, Mac? I left early last year because I was upset when I saw her going off with my boyfriend. Did I miss something?"

Mac gave his big deep rich laugh again.

"You sure did, lovely lady. When Camila has finished with Jeremy she comes hunting for more, both with men and women.

"She goes off like the proverbial box of crackers. No cock or pussy can escape her. And then, when she's had her fill, she will, literally, just disappear."

Lisa and Rosa stared at Mac and then at each other.

"My God, Lisa ? To stay or go, that is the question. Is it better to suffer the cocks and cunts of this outrageous situation or should a modest girl simply leave."

Mac and Rosa laughed heartily.

"Well, I think I'm now at liberty to enjoy my new freedom so I say we stay.

"And Rosa! While our good friend Mac is making up his mind whether to enjoy us or not, I certainly would be happy to walk you to somewhere quiet and encourage you to be free with me. Any chance of that?"

Rosa pulled Lisa close and nibbled her ear and whispered something. Then she looked at Mac and asked if he would let them know when Camila started letting off her crackers.

"We'll be in that little room at the end of the verandah."

"If I can get away for a moment, I'll definitely let you both know. And can I warn you that I could be hunting too, so watch out."

Two lovely ladies had their way with each other and laughingly expressed the thought that they could have saved themselves the trouble with their ex if they had discovered each other in the very beginning.

Lisa and Rosa were intrigued by the similarities in each other. They both kissed each other and fingered each other in an identical fashion.

After a just a short time, they laughed and Rosa suggested that they verbally predict what the other would want to do next. They had so much fun. When Rosa said she wanted to remove Lisa's knickers she discovered Lisa already had her fingers inside her elastic ready to pull them down. When they had both removed each their knickers and licked between each others legs, they were torn between giggling and gasping and they wondered if these similarities that attracted Jeremy to them in the beginning, would be equally attractive to his lover, Camila.

"We could make a date with Camila and find out what she thinks?"

The two were lying back and licking behind each others knees. Then as one, they moved down to lick and nibble each others ankles and then began sucking each others toes.

"You are a wicked woman, Lisa , and I love that idea. From what we've been told, getting her ear might be more difficult than getting under her miniskirt and playing with her pussy. Lets see what happens."

Mac tapped on the sunroom door. "She's here if you two dare come out."

Lisa and Rosa stopped what they were doing and called back. "We're on our way, Mac."

The now two ex girlfriends of Jeremy rejoined the party and as they did so, looked across at Mac. He smiled and nodded his head towards a partly closed door and they headed over to it and quietly entered.

Camila was kneeling on the carpet and she looked amazing. She wore only her stockings and shoes. She was astride a man who had his member in her pussy while at the same time, her plump shapely bottom was being well and truly shagged by two suitors who took turns in her arsehole.

There was something about the woman's body that just demanded attention. She was slightly heavy but very firm. Her well rounded thighs seemed to call out to be touched and fondled and her large stiff nipples could not be ignored by anyones fingers or mouth.

Lisa looked at Rosa. "Will we join them?"

"Oh yes, Lisa. I think we should have our share of the sexy bitch. She owes it to us, after all."

Rosa was first to get her hands on Camila's thighs while Lisa took hold of one of the men working the woman's backside, enjoying her hand movement on the excited bum fucking cock.

The man looked at Lisa and smiled. "Get on your knees and I'll give you some if you want."

Lisa smiled lovingly at him and whispered, "Maybe later. This is fun."

It didn't take Camila long to notice that she had two admiring ladies touching her and she reached out to find their hands and pulled them close.

Then she lifted herself off the cock on the floor and decoupled from the man at the back and suddenly she had her head between Lisa's legs, turning so that Rosa could reach and rub Camila's shaved pussy.

And what a pussy it was. The plumpness of her labia led Rosa to surmise that the woman had opted for some form of surgery. Rosa pushed her face between the large wet slippery folds and inhaled the perfume of the woman's happy cunt. Camila moaned and stretched and pushed herself further into Rosa's face.

Lisa was also moaning as the experienced older woman engulfed her rigid pink cherry and touched it with the end of her tongue. Lisa threw herself upwards and immediately came on the mouth holding her pussy hair tightly between her lips.

Then Camila rolled Lisa over so that she lay on her back on top of Rosa. Then she called the men standing watching.

"Will one of you please fuck this bitch's pussy?"

Camila pushed Lisa's legs apart as the first volunteer presented himself at Lisa 's heavenly gate. Then he pushed in hard and Lisa screamed. "Oh my God! Yes please!"

Camila pushed her mouth on Lisa's mouth and their tongues chased each other around, offering slurping kisses to one another.

Rosa found herself beneath her friend and her suitors thrusting cock and thought she should roll onto her back and join the party. She had no sooner turned and got her hand on the man's bulging testicles than she felt a cock between her own legs and suddenly she joined Lisa and felt a tingling thrill as she was shafted by an excited young man while the voluptuous Camila enjoyed touching both women every which way and wherever she could finger them.

When all the men and been relieved of their cum and had left, the three women lay back and stretched contentedly.

Camila propped herself up on one elbow and stared at Lisa and Rosa. She lazily twirled Lisa's pubic hair around a finger.

"So you were both his girlfriends, I take it? I think I can tell when another woman likes what I like. Am I right? And are you both here to punish me?"

Lisa took Camila's fingers and moved them down and slid them gently into her wet vagina.

"Well, I'm Rosa and I gave Jeremy up a year ago and I believe Lisa here, gave him up tonight. Right Lisa? We're not mad at you, just intrigued by you and your strong sexual attraction. What is your secret weapon, Camila? Please enlighten us."

Camila laughed appreciatively.

"I don't have any secret formula for attracting men but two things seem to work in my favour. Firstly, I simply adore sex of any sort, male or female or trans, young or old and I single-mindedly pursue it. And second, I don't hold back or hide from what I'm wanting.

"Most men, thankfully, are quite respectful of women so that when a woman like me fronts them and wants their cock in my hand and other places, the poor things are into me like I'm the last whore on earth. I love it.

"I suspect that both of you are the same as me but maybe neither of you know it yet. If you are like me then you will soon discover that you both want lots of cock.

"If you are interested, I belong to a swingers club. The members are all sexually active. There are an equal number of men and woman. I can get satisfaction there quite easily. The members are very accepting of different peoples needs.

"You are too young to join being under the entry age of forty-five. However, a number of us have overcome this age problem by holding private parties in our homes. I could invite you along as guests if you are interested. It would be a good introduction to getting multiple men and women.

"I'm also a regular at a private city gang-bang venue run by some women friends, and that can be a fantastic night out.

"The sooner you two ladies recognise your real inner womanly needs the better for everyone.

"Now! While you both consider my offer, I need one of you underneath me and the other straddling my lonely arse while I frig myself. A girl always needs finishing off."

Rosa and Lisa excitedly did what Camila asked, and when she arched her back and screamed her "Yes," the two young woman arched their backs and came at the same time.

In the post-orgasmic silence the girls reflected on what Camila had said.

In a tiny voice, Lisa spoke first.

"Camila?"

"Yes darling?"

"I'd like to try both of those please."

"I would, too, came a whispered voice from Rosa."

"Good! I'll give you my number and you can text me your details. I'll be in touch and let you know where and when the next event is on."

NINE

THE BROOM CUPBOARD

It was something that just happened.

Dave's sexy wife, Helen, who worked in the dinning room had listened to Lisa's bitter complaint about the difficulty of finding a boyfriend who knew how to treat a woman in bed. Helen had laughed and then suggested that if Lisa really wanted to have an adventure, she should visit her husband, Dave in the Broom Cupboard, beneath the main stairs.

Helen smiled lovingly as she promoted her husband's cause.

"Just knock on his door after 5 on a Friday, darling. I promise you won't be disappointed."

Lisa thought hard and long about Helen's suggestion. She knew that Helen was a swinger.

A woman Lisa met at a student conference recently, had mentioned the hot lady in the tiny skirt and heels she'd enjoyed meeting at an end of year office party who said her name was Helen. The woman blushed and confided that after she'd shared and enjoyed a gang bang with the woman, she introduced herself and Helen told her she worked in the canteen at Lisa's university.

Using that story as a confirmation of Helen's wisdom, Lisa decided to just go with the flow and find out more.

When Dave opened the door and ushered her in, Lisa's heart skipped a beat and she knew immediately that she had put herself in a vulnerable situation.

Through an open doorway leading to a tiny room, one of the foreign cleaning ladies was lying back on a mattress with her dress up around her neck and her knickers around one ankle, and her legs apart. The cock of one of the younger maintenance staff was buried deep inside her hairy patch and the woman was yelling something in a her native tongue.

But that wasn't all.

In another room on the opposite side, Lisa recognised one of the art tutors, naked on a bed with one of the larger cleaning ladies almost naked and on top of her and wearing a strap on thingy that she was hungrily shafting the excited skinny tutor with. The tutor whose name was Veronica, was screaming and the woman shafting her was grunting loudly.

And later, when she and Lisa were ending their exciting sexual escapades and the exhausted tutor staggered over and gathered her clothes and began to get dressed, she looked across at Lisa and offered a smile of recognition, acknowledging their complicity in the orgiastic activities that had brought them both to the Broom Cupboard.

Meanwhile, as Lisa excitedly stood and watched these riveting scenes, she felt Dave's hands moving up under her skirt and touching her legs and thighs and just moments later he had dragged Lisa's hand to his exposed penis and she clasped it and gasped and accepted that at long last, she was touching something she knew she had so desperately wanted to get hold of for a very long time; a real man's cock.

Dave backed Lisa up against a wall and dragged down her knickers and palmed her pussy then suddenly Lisa gave a little scream and found herself housing his large member in her vagina and she pushed back against the wall and thrust her abdomen forward and surrendered to the moment. Then Dave was giving it to her just as she had always fantasised getting it and longed for, and Lisa closed her eyes and gasped as Dave rammed her, and all the time she screamed "yes, yes, yes".

Then the door opened and two more male cleaners arrived. They laughed when they saw what Dave was doing and asked if they could try the new girl.

Lisa watched through glazed eyes as the two men unzipped themselves and she stared lustfully at two big red shiny cocks, and it wasn't long before all three men were giving her even more of what she'd long wanted, taking turns and telling her what a wonderful sexy slut she was.

Lisa closed her eyes and she knew she was in cock heaven.

Then other men arrived and joyfully joined in, shagging the ecstatic Lisa with great enthusiasm.

Each one took a turn exploding in her and when Lisa finally staggered from Dave's office with a stream of cum running out of her, she figured that she must have enjoyed at least six different cocks and she had been cream-pied by all of them. And she also knew for certain that she would be back again at the Broom Cupboard next Friday at five o'clock. Lisa would definitely want more of what she'd just had. The newly liberated inner slut knew that it wanted to do it all over again.

Sucking and having multiple cocks have been Lisa's favourite thing in life ever since, when those Friday afternoons in the Broom Cupboard on campus became her essential recreational pastime.

Dave never tired of Lisa and neither did any of the staff, including the big lady with the dildo. Even the non-english speaking ladies would ask in broken english if they could put their heads between her legs after her usual heavy fucking sessions. For Lisa, heaven lived in The Broom cupboard.

Lisa loved who she was and what she did with the people she met, both men and women.

TEN

FEMME TIME

It was a dull normal Tuesday at uni when a bored Lisa wandered into the dining room. It was early afternoon and only a few people were spread around the large area, most of them with books and laptops working on late assignments. Many students had already left for the Christmas holidays.

As she looked around, Lisa noticed the art tutor, Veronica, who she had seen enjoying herself on Fridays at the Broom Cupboard. Neither knew each other to talk to. Veronica was not one of Lisa's tutors.

It was a mixture of boredom and curiosity which led Lisa to approach Veronica as she sat eating a salad role and scanning a magazine.

Veronica looked up and smiled.

"Lisa, isn't it? Like to join me?"

Lisa excused herself to go and fetch a coffee then returned and sat opposite the petite woman. The two looked at each other, each wanting to know more about the other.

Lisa led the way. "God! I just wish it was Friday."

Veronica laughed out loud then added, "I would too except I have something on later today that will get me through until my usual

Friday fun. The person who was to come with me has pulled out. Maybe I should invite you along?"

Lisa was immediately interested.

"Sounds interesting, Veronica. Can I ask what this exciting thing is that you have planned, and more importantly, is it rude?"

Veronica laughed and fixed Lisa with a particular look that assured Lisa that the answer was going to be yes.

Veronica looked around then leant towards Lisa and spoke in a hushed voice.

"I've been invited to be a Cum Queen at a pre Christmas breakup at a business mens club and I need to find a second person. Would you be interested, Lisa ?"

Lisa indicated that she would, "How could I not want to be your partner. It sounds wonderful."

"I'm a close friend of one of the wives who is a swinger and who I know intimately, if you know what I mean.

"Irene is the wife of the club's president. They, and most of the patrons are members of the East Sydney Swingers club. I reckon there will be plenty to go around and enough for the two of us. Oh yes! There will be a lot of women as well. You okay with the girl thing?"

Lisa's mind was racing, partly with excitement for the idea but also the logistics of getting ready and getting there.

"I'm fine with the girl thing, Veronica. Just worried about time and getting myself ready. I'll need to shower and get my slutty stuff on. Thanks for inviting me, by the way. Its sounds just what I'm needing. What time and where?"

Veronica smiled and told her the address which wasn't far from the university accomodation where Lisa lived.

"So glad we met today, Lisa . Now I can look forward to laying down with the slut I always admire on a Friday."

The two laughed and swapped phone numbers.

"Irene's husband's name is Ralph. I don't know anyone else, or at least I don't think I do. Do you have a mask, Lisa? If not I'll bring one for you."

Lisa thanked her and asked if she would bring her a mask, adding that she must go shopping for one. Then they agreed to meet in a small cafe just along from mansion they would be performing in.

"Since I saw you earlier, Lisa , I've been updated. The itinerary now is that we are in a room just off the big room where party goers will swing later.

"The men will not appear until around eleven thirty because they will have their annual meeting and apparently there is a lot of business to get through.

"We will be entertaining the ladies for a couple of hours prior to the mens arrival.

"I'm very happy with this as I can assure you that these women are fun and full on. Being swingers means that at some time or other, they have pretty much all fucked each others husbands and most likely each other.

"They will visit us at around nine. It will be a lot of fun both physically and listening to their stories. The women are great talkers and their stories can be truly hilarious."

Veronica and Lisa took off their skirts and tops and made themselves comfortable on one of two large sofa's in their allocated room. They looked perfect in their heels and stockings, suspender belts and frilly lingerie. Their big lipsticked lips looked forever welcoming to either men or woman.

Before she left, their contact, Irene, remarked on how hot they looked and laughingly said she hope they would have enough energy for the men after the women had had their way with them.

"I don't think we should bother with masks for our girl visitors, Lisa. I'm comfortable with them knowing who I am. But we should apply some lube. The girls can get pretty carried away with their dildos. Most of them wear a standard small one held down by their knickers."

Lisa had been thinking about the next couple of hours and had decided that she was looking forward to it. This amount of attention from women would be a new thing for her and she would probably learn a lot.

Four women arrived through the door together, laughing and commenting about something that they'd been talking about on the way in.

"He'll never work it out, and if he did it wouldn't matter. He heads off to his club early on Thursday afternoons and ten minutes later I arrive and lift my dress over my head and fall between the legs of his secretary. We've been doing that for nearly two years now. We're very close.

"Sometimes I'll meet Erica on her day off and we'll go shopping and she helps me pick out his socks or underpants. Sometimes she'll text me and come to the house and we'll relax near the pool."

Lisa suddenly found herself being held and cuddled by a fine looking woman. Then the woman turned Lisa 's head and kissed her passionately and slipped a hand inside Lisa 's bra and pinched a nipple.

"So you've never been sprung, Charlotte?" asked the woman now removing Lisa's bra.

Charlotte was on the floor, licking Lisa's ankles.

"Actually, we were a couple of months ago, Margaret. The tea-lady, Grace, barged in on us looking for her car keys when Erica was on top of me.

"The poor woman didn't know what to do or say but we fixed that by laughing and saying it was okay. We reached up and drew down her big knickers over her large backside and her solid stockinged legs. The poor woman was beside herself with feelings of both fear and excitement.

"Grace settled down once I had her big bushy cunt in my hand. Then we laid her on the carpet and Erica and I took turns in shagging the sweet lady who was soon wrapping her legs around our waists and pulling us closer.

"She was gasping and touching us all over and asking for more. We decided to give it to her hard which was a good thing because she suddenly exploded.

"When she'd caught her breath, Grace laughed and blushed and mumbled a "thank you". Then she informed us that we had given her the best shagging she'd ever experienced; better even than when Father Patrick used to come around to their house and spend half the night shagging her and her mum, when Grace was just nineteen.

"She added that the priest particularly liked having her half laying on the bed with her legs wide apart while he preferred her mum against the wall with her backside facing out and giving it to her doggy fashion.

"We asked how long this had gone on for and Grace blushed even more and added that the last time Father Patrick got between her and her mum's legs was on her wedding day.

"He had called around in the morning to check we were all set for the big event. Mum was so excited about the wedding, she pushed father Patrick down on the kitchen floor and opened his trousers and the two of us took turns riding him.

"It really got us going and that night I wouldn't let my husband stop fucking me.

"My mother set her self up in the garden where the wedding reception was being held and fucked my new husbands father, the best man and whoever else she could get her hands on.

"She and I both agreed that Father Patrick had been the tonic we both needed."

Lisa was fascinated that the women who were giving her so much attention were at the same time, carrying on far reaching conversations. She thought how this was living proof that women could do more than one thing as a time.

Lisa's bra was gone as were her knickers. The woman had laid her back against the back of the sofa and was now kneeling and feasting noisily between Lisa's legs.

"Is that as tasty as it looks, Margaret? Move over darling and let me have some."

All of Lisa's senses were alive. What was happening to her and the story she had listened to had fired her up.

She suddenly shook and shuddered and rolled over and pushed her pussy up against Margaret's thigh.

"Oh you are a darling young thing. Did you feel that, Charlotte?"

After her mini orgasm, Lisa managed a moments respite, long enough to look for Veronica.

Her friend was up against the wall and totally naked apart from her stockings and her shoes. Three more women had arrived and now five ladies wielded their dildos, were taking turns with the petite Veronica.

Lisa saw that the look on her friend's face showed that she was very happy. She seemed to have things under control. As each woman had her turn from the front, Veronica would swivel around and push out her butt.

Then Lisa's ladies were talking again.

"Lets roll her over, Margaret. I want to see her butt."

Lisa obliged by languidly rolling over onto her stomach and stretching her legs towards her suiters, displaying her neat derriere.

"Oh God! Look at this gorgeous young bum, Charlotte. I'd love to have a go at that."

Lisa turned her head and looked back at the two randy women and smiled.

"I'd love it if you did, ladies. It's one of my favourite things, and it can take a pounding if you want to get energetic."

No more words were needed. Charlotte repositioned Lisa on the sofa so that she knelt on the carpet with her bum in the air.

"Oh God! This is just what a girl needs. And look, she's already lubed it."

For the next ten minutes, Charlotte and Margaret plugged Lisa's bottom with their equipment. But not only that, as one entered Lisa, the other put her dildo into the backside of her friend, vigorously heaving herself at the welcoming pink hole buried between the friends buttocks.

Charlotte and Margaret were in heaven and when they allowed themselves to orgasm, Lisa came with them.

They smothered Lisa with kisses and sucked on her tongue.

"Thank you darling. That might be the highlight of the night, Margaret. Maybe we should come back for more later."

As the two women lay back for a moments rest, Lisa knelt between them, fondling and kissing a breast on each and smiling at their satisfied faces. Then she laughed and took each woman's hand and kissed it.

"You are wonderful lovers. You know how to make a girl feel good. I'm yours whenever you want me. Come back later and bring your husbands with you if you like."

For the next hour, women came through the door in two's and three's and sometimes more.

It seemed that word had spread and every female in attendance wanted to try the Cum Queens.

As soon as they spotted Lisa and Veronica laying back with their charms on display, they set upon them with gusto, dragging them to the carpet and slipping their dildos into them and into each other wherever they could. It could only be likened to a more gentle and consensual gang-bang and Lisa and Veronica enjoyed it as just that.

And the snippets of conversation continued to entertain.

A bosomy woman and her slender chest-challenged friend took hold of Lisa and Veronica and lovingly put their heads between their legs while continuing their ongoing stories each time they lifted their heads for air.

"My daughter in-law came to me and complained that my son was not showing her enough attention. Paul is a stockbroker who works on the trading room floor and he comes home exhausted each night.

"Courtney said she knew that I was a member of the East Sydney Swingers Club and wondered if joining it would help solve her problems.

"Courtney is the typical trophy wife, a tall, slim and beautiful blond.

"I told her that she was too young and would need to wait at least another ten years before she could become a member to which she replied that the way things were with her and Paul, I probably wouldn't be her mother-in-law by then.

"Then I told her I'd see what I could do."

The two women stopped what they were doing and agreed to change over and Lisa suddenly found her hands being moved to hold on to the big breasted ladies breasts as the woman gurgled in Lisa's wet vagina.

Then she surfaced, licked her lips and continued talking.

"I talked to some of the older men in the club who were retired and no longer went to the office during the week. Then I came up with a plan.

"I told Courtney that I may have solved her problem and she should come around the next day at around two o'clock. I also told her to dress in her sexiest gear.

"I'd instructed Mrs Maitland – a young widow and my part-time housekeeper – to help me move the little day bed into the alcove beside the dining room, then I put a couple of those acrylic faux-fur mats beside the bed and pulled the big curtain across to provide a little privacy.

"When Courtney arrived a little early as instructed, I told her that I had arranged for a dozen Swingers Club members to come around for a luncheon smorgasbord and with something special on the side. I showed her the little bed and I told her she was to be the something on the side.

"She was wildly excited and flung her arms around me. She looked really good and I fancied her myself. I think Mrs Maitland did too, and I got the feeling that Courtney would have taken whatever sexual attention she could get."

Lisa and Veronica were loving this story and didn't want it to end.

Then Veronica had a good idea to keep the woman close so that they could continue with the story and she spoke with her poor little girl voice.

"We would love it if you two ladies could shag us with your dildos. Pretty please?"

The two suitors were momentarily silent and stared at Veronica and Lisa, then without missing hardly a beat in their conversation, the two pushed into them with their brightly coloured dildo thingy's and Big Breasts continued with her story.

"Well, to cut the story short, it was Courtney that made the first move, taking two of the men by their hands and. Swaying seductively on her long bare legs and expensive black and silver Bruno Magli heeled sandals, she led them behind the curtain. Moments later there was a scream and then all we heard was "Yes, oh, yes, yes please. Please don't stop!"".

Lisa ventured to acknowledge the woman's story by laughing and saying how she had enjoyed listening to the big breasted lady as much as she had enjoyed her physical attention between her legs.

The big lady laughed and looked down at the smiling woman beneath her and slipped fingers into Lisa's welcoming pussy.

"Well, darling that is not the end of the story.

"I hadn't really anticipated how it would all play out. I hadn't allowed for the possibility of the other men wanting anything other than the beautiful Courtney behind the curtain. But they did.

"When Mrs Maitland came in to clear the dishes and I went to help her, we both found that we had arms around us and hands wandered over our chests and backsides. Men were smiling at us all around and they were soon taking off our clothes.

"I looked across at Mrs Maitland and inquired if this was all right, considering she was only working here and had not volunteered for any of the fun and games. But as one man held up her skirt and another slipped his hand down inside her big knickers and had taken hold of her large hairy pussy; and while another unhitched her bra, a flushed Mrs M smiled coyly and gasped that she was "just fine thank you".

"The two of us very quickly found ourselves being dragged behind the curtain and laid down alongside the bed where Courtney was gurgling with satisfaction as her two suitors took turns between her legs.

"Mrs Maitland blubbered excitedly when she saw the beautiful Courtney laying back with her legs wide apart and being heartily shafted and calling out.

"But Mrs M was very quickly silenced when a cock slipped in between her lips and as she felt two more sets of hands removing her knickers.

"I too, had surrendered to my seducers, most of whom I had

enjoyed on numerous occasions at swingers club functions and as they fondled my pussy and removed my clothes I certainly wasn't going to protest. This was going to be a much better smorgasbord than I ever expected.

"Over the next hour or more, the beautiful Courtney managed to accomodate and enjoy all twelve men, and she obviously loved it. She even started calling out "Whose next?" and dragging nearby cocks into her wide open mouth while enthusiastically fingering their testicles.

"Her beautiful legs seemed to be permanently waving in the air with men wildly catching them and smothering them with kisses and licking her behind her knees.

"Some rubbed their cocks against her feet while they waited their turn at her pussy and one foot fetishist even ejaculated all over her red painted toes.

"When Mrs Maitland and I found ourselves bent over on top of the beauty while we were happily being shafted from the back, Courtney put her hands on our tits and touch our pussies and squeeze the testicles of our providers of pleasure.

"When everyone had left, Courtney lay on the bed with her eyes closed and a smile on her face. A hand moved backwards and forward between her legs, then she lifted her fingers to her mouth and leisurely licked them. She had discovered that she like the taste of cum and wanted more of it.

"Then she lifted her head and smiled and sobbed and told me that she was keeping me as her mother-in-law for ever.

"It was then that I realised that I'd probably saved my sons marriage and with the beautiful creature now sitting on my face, I knew that I would be there to help my daughter-in-law whenever she needed me.

"From that day on, Courtney's needs were met each month as I provided her with another smorgasbord. She never tired of it and Mrs Maitland and myself didn't either.

"Oh yes, and Mrs Maitland went on a diet, bought new clothes and joined the Sydney Swingers club.

When the succession of excited females slowed and then stopped, Veronica slumped down beside Lisa on the settee and the two touched each other and kissed and congratulated one another on a job well done.

"Well, Veronica. I guess we'll be seeing the men soon. But now that I've met so many of the swinging ladies and seen how active they are, I'm wondering why they ordered a pair of Cum Queens? It's not as though there is a shortage of women who will happily open their legs for any mans offering. They all seem to be up for it. So why bring us in? Have I missed something?"

Veronica settled back and pondered what Lisa had said.

"I know what you mean, Lisa, and I've been wondering the same thing and I've been thinking about Irene.

"I first met her at an end of year office orgy. There were about sixty people and the sexes were split around fifty-fifty. The women were mainly office workers and secretaries. Irene was there with her husband.

"There were a number of rooms and when I explored I discovered Irene in a small staff room.

"She was stripped down to her undies and was sporting a small dildo, the sort we've seen here today that fit into the owners vagina. She was sharing a half-a-dozen or more young office workers with a girl friend who was also equipped with a dildo.

"I could not be certain whether the office girls had taken or been given a substance of some kind, but they were all frantically trying to get their pussy's filled by the two older woman with the pretend cocks, screaming out that it was their turn.

"I didn't see Irene with a man the entire evening. And when I called back to that room much later, Irene and her friend had given their dildos to the young women who were now taking it in turns to shag the two older women, screaming with excitement as Irene and her friend rubbed and sucked the girls vaginas in return.

"Which brings me to the present, Lisa.

"Irene was only here for a very short time today because she said that she had an appointment elsewhere but I have heard that she expressed to a friend on the phone that she hoped they would enjoy that special something she had organised for the girls. I now believe that was us, hidden behind the Cum Queen label supposedly meant for the men but actually intended for the rampant Femme side of the group.

"In short, we were brought her for the woman and between you and me, I'm happy about that."

Lisa thought about what Veronica had said.

"If that is the case, Veronica, and we're not going to be entertaining the fellas, and if we'd like some cock on the side, so to speak, I vote we get dressed and just go and join the swingers out through that door."

Veronica laughed and kissed Lisa on her belly.

"I fully agree. Lets do that, Lisa. I would like a nice cock before I leave. But of course we might get caught by our randy women friends from earlier. Let's wear our masks and see what happens. Those women can be addictive but a nice big red hot juicy cock would be a welcome change."

ELEVEN
WHEN OLD IS YOUNG

Jessica was asked by Maude if she would help out with a couple of the pre Christmas musical commitments that she had made.

The church choir leader had the bright idea that it would be good for its members to perform in front of an audience to get experience. Jessica was to join two other's to visit retirement villages and give a concert during the late afternoon after residents had had their nap.

Their first gig was at The Willows, a village for wealthy retirees, situated on the coast just below Bondi. The residents loved what the choir members did which was a medley of songs from the 40's and 50's and everyone applauded and asked for more.

When the trio finished, the young man and woman who were a couple, downed their soft-drinks and cake and left as quickly as they could, citing another engagement further down the coast.

As Jessica finished her slice of apple cake, a couple of residents who were still at the table smiled at her and the well groomed woman with bright eyes asked Jessica if she would come to their unit for dinner the night after next. With nothing planned and not giving things much thought, Jessica agreed and when she asked what she could bring to the meal, the woman assured her that just bringing herself, would be quite sufficient.

Jessica made the short bus trip to a stop near The Willows and when she arrived, her hosts, Angela and Craig, said how very pleased they were that she had found her way there and how excited they were to see her. The unit was very beautiful and much bigger than Jessica had anticipated, boasting three bedrooms and a study as well as the lounge and a large dining alcove.

The good looking couple must have been in their mid sixty's or a little older. He was partially deaf and when his wife asked him why he wasn't wearing his hearing aids, he just answered that he couldn't find them. As a result, Craig didn't have a lot to say because he wasn't able to follow the conversation.

Jessica at first felt a little self-conscious, intending to dress more casually, she ended up confused and settled for a smart conservative look. She settled for a tight black skirt with a white blouse, tan stocking and standard shiny-black low heels. Angela was also smartly dressed in fashionable clothes including black stockings and low heels.

The meal was excellent and Jessica enjoyed the opportunity to relax in pleasant company and enjoy a glass of wine; a white sauterne which went well with the poached fish.

When they eventually moved back into the softer light of the lounge room and sat back on the sofa and arm chairs, they swapped stories about family and their childhood upbringing and then slowly moved on to talk about their daily lives.

Craig must have realised that he was missing out on most of what was being said and rose, and excused himself, announcing that he was going in search of his missing hearing aids.

Jessica smiled at him and wished him luck, thinking what a fit and good looking couple these two older folk were.

"I would assume that an attractive young woman like yourself would have a partner?" asked Angela with a knowing smile when they were suddenly alone.

Jessica laughed and replied that, no she hadn't settled on the right man or woman yet and was very happily enjoying herself and playing the field.

Angela looked pleasantly surprised and smiled and looked at Jessica closely, then chose her words carefully.

"Can I confide in you Jessica?"

Jessica was slightly taken aback, wondering what sort of things, Angela – a mature woman – had to confide in to someone much younger.

"Of course you can, Angela, but I'm not sure whether I'm a person who can be of much help. I'll soon let you know if I can or can't."

At that moment, Craig came back into the lounge room.

"Found them! Now I'm just popping up to the corner shop for more wine, darling. We're out of everything and we'll need some for tomorrow when the kids come for lunch. See you both shortly."

The two women farewelled him and Angela told him not to get lost, fixing him with a stern stare.

"I have a feeling that Craig is spending time with another woman, darling. I know I shouldn't burden you with this but I really don't have anyone outside the family or neighbours to talk to and the subject is too delicate anyway."

Angela asked Jessica to come over and join her on the sofa. Then she took Jessica's hands in hers and looked deep into her eyes.

"There's a new woman at number forty-nine. Robyn is her name. She is quite a hit with the men in the street and I'm sure some of the other wives are having the same trouble as me.

"Robyn has a woman friend visit her regularly and the two of them seem to attract the men like flies to a honey-pot. I don't know what they all get up to but it certainly keeps the men knocking on her door."

Jessica noticed that Angela had moved one of her hands onto Jessica's knee and was absentmindedly caressing it with her finger tips, as she spoke. It felt very nice and Jessica decided to take a risk.

"Have you ever been with a woman, Angela? I have a woman lover as well as male friends. I find being with a woman is emotionally very rewarding."

Angela's jaw dropped as she thought through what Jessica had just said. Then she rallied herself and with her eyes downcast, she whispered that she hadn't ever been with a woman in that way but it was something she had thought about often over the years. Angela looked up as Jessica replied.

"I find you very attractive, Angela. Would you let me kiss you? It's all right to say no. Its just that I love everything about you. Just one kiss will do?"

Angela was flustered and didn't know where to look. She put her other hand on Jessica's thigh. Then she rallied, made the decision and looked at Jessica.

"We will have to be quick, before Craig gets home," then she closed her eyes and lent forward, pushing her lips out towards Jessica.

Jessica smiled and before she moved in to kiss Angela, said. "From what you have told me, I suspect your husband might enjoy seeing two women kissing."

Angela's lips touched Jessica's and the woman sat frozen in time. Then Jessica moved her lips around a little, trying to encourage Angela to participate. Then she took Angela's hand from her thigh and lifted it and put it on a breast, rotating it gently. Finally, she moved the hand on her knee up under her skirt until it touched the soft flesh above her stockings. It was then that Angela pushed her mouth against Jessica's and pushed her tongue in between Jessica's lips, making little breathless sounds indicating her excitement.

"We have lift off," Jess thought as she moved her own hand up under Angela's skirt and felt a warm spot at the top of her legs buried beneath Angela's knickers.

Angela was enlivened, throwing her arms around Jessica and falling backwards and pulling the young woman on top of her. Then just as quickly, she unbuttoned her blouse, pulled her breasts out from her bra, and pushed Jessica's head down to suck her nipples.

"Oh Jessica this is wonderful and you are wonderful. Please keep kissing me."

"Yes, this is wonderful Angela. I'm so loving it, too."

Jessica felt Angela's hand unzipping the back of her skirt and smiled when the woman's fingers found the crack in her buttocks. Angela's hand didn't stop there. It slid down to the back of her legs then pushed forward gently and discovering Jessica's wet pussy.

Angela sighed and pushed her lips hard against Jessica's and joined the young woman in a tongue dance. Jessica remembered that she had an urgent question for Angela and pulled her head up and looked at her.

"I do just have one important question relating to your husband, though, Angela. Tell me, do you ever suck his penis?

Jessica looked down at Angela's face which bore a look of amazement.

"Well, no I don't. My mother taught all four daughters never to touch a man there because it wasn't a nice thing to do. Strangely, whilst it's crossed my mind on occasion, I haven't had the courage to go against my mothers advice. Why do you ask?"

"It's one of the main things that women can do to keep their husbands from going elsewhere."

Jessica listened for an answer and in response to Angela's silence, except for her heavy breathing, went back to kissing her breasts while at the same time pushing her hand up hard against Angela's vagina, sheltering behind the crotch of her tights and underpants.

"I really want to taste you between your legs, Angela. I'm taking off your knickers. Okay?"

"Please do, Jessica. This is all like a dream. I love it."

Jessica first removed her own skirt and then lifted Angela up and began to drag her tights down over her legs. It was when she had them down around the woman's knees, that she heard voices. It was far too late for a cover up.

Craig had brought two mates home for a drink and a supper snack and to meet their nice young visitor.

He'd met the men in the street on his way home from the shops and when his friends were just arriving home from golf. One was a married man who's wife happened to be away for a week, visiting one of their children. The other was a widower. All played golf together and as it happened, all visited the new woman, Robyn, at number forty-nine.

When Craig and his friends looked at what was happening on the sofa, none could believe their eyes, especially, Craig.

Angela looked up at the shocked faces of the men and found herself smiling. She had been liberated from so much in just such a short time by Jessica's loving touch, and without stopping to think,

Angela called out, "We're having a party if any of you gentlemen would like to join us."

The three men stared at the two women. Angela had her breasts on show and her legs were together to facilitate her tights being removed.

"This lovely lady, gentlemen, is Jessica. As you can see, we are quite busy, but don't think you have to leave. We will happily deal with you all in a little while. Is that right Jessica? And Jessica, the good looking one in the blue trousers is Norman and the other good looking one is Matt. The other good looking one is my husband who you've already met."

Jessica turned and looked at the three well dressed and fit looking older men.

"Hello everyone. Pleased to meet you. Angela and I will certainly be happy for you to join in our fun. Why don't you all get your cocks out and warm up? We won't be too long and we are happy for you to watch."

Jessica returned to what she was doing and finished pulling off Angela's tights. Then she reached up and removed the woman's panties, deliberately throwing them towards her husband, Craig.

Jessica now buried her head between the top of Angela's legs and licked the woman and nibbled at her clitoris. Angela sighed and closed her eyes and pushed herself up towards Jessica's face while rubbing her breasts.

Loud whispering ensued as the men excitedly talked among themselves while staring at the wondrous scene in front of them, and one by one they surrendered to Jessica's suggestion and got out their penises and began stroking them.

Jessica lifted herself up and moved up and laid on Angela and looked lovingly into the woman's smiling eyes. Angela looked back and puckered up and the two kissed.

"In a few minutes, Angela, I'm going to let you watch me suck cock. Later, you might like to forget the one piece of bad advice your mother ever gave you, and join me.

"Cock sucking is one of my favourite hobbies Angela, and it's very healthy for girl, for both the mind and her body. I won't mind if you don't suck them. You can just play with them and rub them if you like.

But watch me anyway, and see what I do. Is that okay, you sexy woman?"

Angela laughed. "Sounds wonderful, Jessica. I'm desperate to learn more."

"Oh yes, there is just one more thing Angela. These gentlemen will probably want more than me sucking them and will probably want to put their cocks between both our legs.

"Are you okay with me letting Craig pop his member into me, Angela? Just say if you're not and I'll make sure he doesn't. Hopefully your Craig will soon learn the benefits of being at home with his newly liberated woman. What you do with any of other two is your call."

Angela hugged Jessica tightly then ran her hands gently over her body. "God, you sexy little bitch. I want everything. Now! And in answer to your question, do whatever you want to with Craig. I'm sure I will love watching you."

Jessica felt hands on her buttocks and experienced the thrill she always felt when touched ahead of a sexual encounter, instinctively knowing that things were about to happen. She turned her head and saw three erections standing in a row in front of the sofa then Jessica whispered to Angela that she should put her arm out and grab the nearest one and not worry about who it was attached to. Then she continued, "I'm greedy so I'll have two."

Angela giggled at Jessica's comments and immediately pushed her arm out and took a cock in her hand. Then, as Jessica moved away to sit up, Angela swung herself round to a sitting position and looked up to see who lived on the end of what she was holding, and Jessica heard an excited and breathless little voice.

"Hello Norman. You won't mind if I have a play with this, will you?"

"Well done Angela," thought Jessica. "You're on your way."

Jessica looked up at Craig who seemed confused, staring first at Jessica and then at his wife and what she was doing with Norman.

Jessica looked up at Matt, the widower, whose cock seemed the most impressive by size.

"Lovely cocks, gentlemen. I'd love to get to know them better. I hope you won't object if I do."

Jessica looked up at the two men with her sweet coy and oh-so-innocent smile. Then she a visualised a memorable scene; that moment not long ago when her first two stiff cocks presented themselves, swaying and lifting up and down beside her just outside the passenger door window at her first dogging session with her friend in Goulburn. And that same little voice inside Jessica screamed with delight.

Jessica reached out and took hold of Craig's cock. It instinctively jumped up and down in her hand and she fondled it lovingly.

"A girl just can't help herself at a moment like this, Craig. I might get carried away and lick and suck you both. Is that okay? Tell me to stop if you're not happy."

As she spoke, her words caused the two cocks to jump upwards. With her other hand Jessica took hold of Matt and she began a slow rubbing motion on the two of them.

Jessica played with her two cocks for a few minutes, rubbing her fingers lovingly over their hoods and tickling their testicles, then one after the other she took turns feeding them in between her lips and slowly licking and sucking them. When Jessica chanced a look over at Angela she discovered that the woman had indeed watched Jessica and was now busily sucking Norman whose face showed a level of ecstasy that Jessica hadn't seen in a man for a long time.

Angela looked as though she was truly enjoying herself and Jessica recalled the first time that she and Edith and Rosa had laid on the bed in a cool room on a hot summers day and discovered one another, and how the world had been the better for it ever since.

Jessica was loving having access to cocks again. It had only been a couple of weeks since her wonderful sex filled holiday at Goulburn but she still felt as though she hadn't had a proper cock in ages.

Jessica had still to experience being fucked and enjoying it with as much pleasure as her sucking provided. But she did like it and was aware that fucking was what men ultimately felt was their reason for being. For that reason she considered it important to make it available to them. It was important for her not to be selfish.

Encouraging men to have their way was a form of insurance. Being certain that they would be happy to be sucked again was assured when they knew they would be the beneficiaries of a full service afterwards.

Jessica remembered that thing that Gina had said the evening they were dogging in Goulburn. "I'm going to open the door on the other side shortly. I need to offer my other end. The boys deserve the full menu."

After quite sometime in cock play, Jessica decided it was time to move on to fucking mode. But before she did, she wanted to do one thing.

"Angela? Can I have a turn with Norman please? Lets swap places. Angela nodded her agreement without letting go of Norman's cock and Jessica stood up and walked around the back of her two men and behind Norman, and Angela moved over.

Angela soon had a two cocks to deal with, one being her husbands. Without missing a beat, she smiled up at Craig and Matt and took turns feeding them into her mouth, slurping generously on both of them.

Around ten or fifteen minutes after the change over, Jessica whispered as best she could to Angela that she was about to get onto her knees and show the boys what she was offering next on the menu. Angela almost choked laughing. "I'll watch and then I might do the same," she replied.

Jessica stopped sucking Norman and looked up at him.

"I fancy you in a different spot now, Norman. Hope you will be happy with it."

Then Jessica stood and turned around and knelt on the sofa, displaying her beautiful backside and her little vagina.

All the men looked at Jessica's rear end, and as they did so, Angela took the opportunity to do what Jessica had just done. She turned and perched on the edge of the sofa on her knees and displaying her well proportioned womanly bum and a hairy vagina. Jessica noticed and instructed the men accordingly.

"We are offering unrestricted access here today. Please enjoy yourselves, gentlemen. We certainly will."

There was a sudden rush. Three cocks and only two pussies.

Craig plunged his member into his wife without further ado and

Norman took a slow easy approach to pussy poking at Jessica's already wet rear end.

Angela kindly called to Matt to come and sit beside her so that she could rub and play with him to which he acted swiftly, accepting her kind offer.

Having her husband shagging her in front of his mates, excited Angela for some reason she couldn't quite understand. Was it to do with her sudden arrival into a world of more honest interactions. Was him fucking her in this situation like what it was going to be for them both from now on. Was she conscious that this was likely to be the successful way of weaning him away from that tart up the road? She did love him, and hoped all of these things were true. Then she smiled to herself and the new Angela thought how nice it would be to fuck his two friends before the night was over.

Other mens cocks were probably the last essential ingredient in Angela's liberation.

Jessica had considered the lack of condoms but dismissed it as a concern, telling herself that these men were probably clean and she had been for a check-up this week and was fine.

Funny how we tell ourselves reassuring things when it suits us, she mused.

Craig came quite quickly and Angela felt a huge load slipping around in her and unusually, she experienced small orgasmic tremors in her genitals. Her husband bellowed like a bull and everyone smiled.

As her husband left her, she looked up and smiled and blew him a kiss. Then she turned to Matt.

"I'd would love it if you fucked me too, Matt. But only if you want to."

Matt was up and at her in just moments, and Craig turned and watched in awe.

"Oh, Matt how kind of you. Give it to me like it's your last one ever, Matt, and I'll make you your favourite chocolate cake tomorrow."

What more of an incentive could a man ask for, Jessica smiled to herself, overhearing Angela's offer. Then she thought about not having made a chocolate cake for ages and that she, being once the top cake maker of her final school year, should surprise Edith with one next week.

Norman came with a bleating sound accompanied by what sounded like a last gasp.

"Thank you Norman. Craig? You've given it all to that other slut. But perhaps you could manage to give me a little touch up, please?"

Craig stepped forward and put his hand between Jessica's legs and fingered her very wet pussy. She returned the favour by gently rubbing his balls. Then she took his hand in hers and pushed three of his fingers into her vagina really hard and moved them vigorously, in and out. Then Jessica uttered a little scream and came on Craig's hand.

"Thank you Craig. Just what I needed."

The men stood or sat around, a little dazed and unsure of themselves, like boys thinking they were still about to get into trouble for what they had been doing. But then Angela put her arms around her husband who sat on the floor in front of her, and nibbled his ear.

"Thank you darling. What a wonderful husband you are. Hope you liked it. Just ask when you want some more. I'm here for you darling, whenever and for whatever you want me for. Oh, and darling, I'll want to suck your cock at least twice a day from now on. I've decided that I love it."

Jessica laughed and looked at the other two men and said how she thought that they were pretty good too.

There wasn't a lot to chat about at that moment, so Jessica thought she should say something.

"Thank you all. I really enjoyed your company tonight and want to thank Angela for making it possible. At the risk of looking stupid, would you raise your hands if you feel you would like to do it all again sometime. If Angela and Craig are willing of course, I will happily come over to their house and take off my knickers for another romp."

Everyone put their hand up then Jessica looked at Angela.

"I look forward to hearing from you, Angela."

When the men had shuffled off home, or in Craig's case, farewelling Jessica and excused himself and headed off to bed, the two women reached out for each other and kissed then rolled onto the sofa together.

"Oh, my God, Jessica, life will never be the same again, thanks to you."

Jessica moved quickly, putting her head down between Angela's legs and slurping up the cream pies the two lovely men had left behind and which were now beginning to dribble from her new love. This was nectar to the extraordinary cock loving Jessica. Then just as she was finishing and about to take her mouth away, she felt Angela stiffen and realised that the woman's pussy was looking for more.

With three deft fingers and a thumb, Jessica gave Angela her first proper orgasm in a long time, enjoying the moment when Angela arched her back and screamed out. Then she held her in her arms while the newly liberated lovely lady sobbed and placed sloppy kisses all over any part of Jessica she could reach.

The two settled down and rested in each others arms.

"Angela?"

"Yes, Jessica?"

"Did you like sucking cock, darling?"

"Loved it!"

"And being fucked by other cocks?"

"Loved it!"

"Make a habit of it, Angela. It will keep you young."

TWELVE
A SMORGASBORD

Jessica visited her new friends, Angela and husband Craig, every six or eight week at their unit at The Willows, a retirement village for well off retirees. It wasn't that she wouldn't have liked to see more of them, it was to do with the amount of time available to her, what with work and her other activities.

Enjoying herself at Angela's place was most exciting for both the good food and the company as well as the sex with neighbours, usually the same two men plus Craig.

Jessica was Angela's first female sex partner and her coming out and her liberation meant that she was keen to catch up on those things in life that she thought she had missed out on. So when Angela called her and asked her if she was up for a visit and something a little different, Jessica jumped at the opportunity.

"I hope its still rude, whatever it is, Angela?" Jessica asked, laughingly.

"Definitely!" Angela assured her.

"Are you going to give me a hint, at least, you super sexy senior slut?"

Angela laughed. She loved it when Jessica called her a senior slut. It sounded like she was the holder of an important position in life, and Jessica assured her that indeed, it was very important.

"If I said there would be a lot more cocks and probably extra women, would that interest you, my ravishing super slut?"

Jessica was immediately excited and screamed her answer into the telephone.

"God yes, Angela. I'm looking for my lubricant as we speak. Are the ladies experienced, can I ask, or do we have to introduce them to the better things of life?"

Angela screamed back her amusement.

"Well, Jessica, it seems that, unbeknown to me, there are quite a number of swinging residents here at the village and also among other members of Craig's golfing fraternity. He says there are at least half a dozen bringing their partners who will no doubt be expecting to have a good time with each others husbands.

"Robyn, our honeypot from number 49 wants to join us. She's already visited me during an afternoon when Craig was at golf. If I just tell you that we got on famously, you will get the picture."

Jessica feigned disapproval.

"You dirty little slut, you. Do I have to share you now with an experienced bisexual superstar who lives practically on the premises? How will I ever be able to compete?"

"Oh you are a darling. I think you will like her. And if you don't, well you can fight it out between sucking and fucking all the men and women that are coming. Half the golf club apparently, if Craig isn't exaggerating."

"Well, bitch. I'll certainly be there to compete for cocks with the two of you. So watch out!"

Jessica made a point of being late. It wasn't something she would normally do but there was method in her madness. She knew that making a late entrance would get her the most attention and dressed in her sluttiest clothes, she knew she would get an interesting reception.

Strangely, it wasn't the men she wanted to impress the most, it was the honeypot woman, Robyn. If it came to a cock sucking stand-off, Jessica wanted to win. Then she reminded herself that she was being foolish; and then she reminded herself again that she was going there to have fun. There was nothing to fight over.

Angela and Craig's apartment was crowded. Everyone was still going through the niceties of greeting each other and asking after each others health. But a few that had got there early and had a glass of wine, were already showing signs of wanting to try out with someone.

Jessica found Angela and they kissed and then Angela took her and introduced her to Robyn who immediately put an arm around Jessica's waist and pulled her close. Then she kissed her on the lips saying how Angela had told her all about her tall young friend.

But there was too much going on and too much noise for anyone to have a proper conversation.

Jessica told her host that she would like to have a little wander about on her own to get the feel of things and Angela smiled and replied that the sooner people started feeling things, the better.

Hansome well dressed men and women were everywhere and Jessica thought how much they reminded her of the crowd at the dunking near Goulburn she had been to with Gina and Darlene.

Not everyone was in the same mold, however. In the kitchen she discovered a huge blond woman in a bright floral kaftan and with bare feet, wearing her hair braided like she had just stepped off the plane from Bali.

She wore blue eyeshadow and pale pink lipstick and her varnished finger and toe nails were pink. She spoke with a Dutch accent and threw her arms around any man that came within touching distance, kissing him passionately and telling him with only a slight slur in her guttural accented voice, that she hoped he would favour her body before the night was out. They would each murmur something back which Jessica couldn't catch accept that the woman's name sounded like Dunya.

"Well, that will be interesting," thought Jessica, looking at the woman. She would surely have been six-foot three or four and had a huge backside and enormous breasts.

In the passageway that led to the toilet, a couple where in each others arms and kissing passionately. In the lounge, men and women were talking and laughing and quite a few men and some women were rubbing someone's rear end, affectionately as part of a preliminary signalling.

It wasn't until she looked into the first of the dimly lit bedrooms that she saw things we're really starting to get under way.

A good looking well built man was leaning against a wardrobe door with his trousers and pants down around his ankles. Two women knelt in front of him sucking what looked to be a sizeable and happy cock, and passing it backwards and forwards to each other. One woman had a hand between the others legs who in turn, was slowly unbuttoning the shirt of the woman feeling her up. Jessica response was to put her own hand down and slide her fingers up under her mini skirt. She would have liked to join in but thought she would keep looking around before making any moves.

As she turned to leave the room, a smiling woman entered followed closely by two men. The woman had a cock in each hand and headed to the double bed. Then she stopped and let their cocks go while she lifted her dress up over her head and then unfastened her bra and let it drop to the floor.

Then the woman rolled over onto her knees and pushed her rear end provocatively towards the two men and Jessica heard her speak in a low sensuous voice, "Who wants to be first?"

Jessica couldn't help but feel horny. But she was determined to have a good look around. She still had two bedrooms to look in plus the dining room.

In the second bedroom, at first she thought it was empty, but then she heard sounds coming from the carpeted floor on the other side of the bed and tippy-toed across and peeped.

She was surprised but enchanted with the hot scene that confronted her, and what was said was even more exciting.

A woman was on her knees with her dress up over her shoulders and her kickers own around her ankles and her bare bum in the air. A second woman wearing a dildo was shagging the first woman's vagina energetically, and talking in a breathless voice.

"I know you've been fucking him in our shed on the days I'm at work, for bloody ages, you bitch. But all along, it was me that you were really after, wasn't it? Wasn't it? Bitch? This is what you really wanted, wasn't it? Well, now you've go me and I'll expect more of this, you dirty little husband fucking whore.

From now on you will come to my place on a Wednesday afternoon when my Mervyn's at golf and get what I'm giving you now. And you are going to have to fuck me too. Have you got that, slut?"

A weak sobbing voice answered. "Oh, yes, Susan, oh yes. Just keep shagging me, Susan. Please don't stop. I want it! I've always wanted this. And yes, Susan, I'll come to your place on a Wednesday and you can fuck me as much as you like."

Jessica was rubbing herself furiously, wanting to be both the fucker and the fuckee. She made a mental note of what the two women wearing incase she ran across them again later.

Bedroom three, and what a scene. Two men were holding a women up off the floor, each with a shapely leg over their respective elbows. Her arms held each man by the neck. All her clothing had been removed except for her stockings and suspender belt and heels. A third man was fucking her enthusiastically, yelling that he was about to come. The woman screamed her satisfaction then let herself down from the two men while they changed places and the next man fucked her equally enthusiastically.

When this third man finished, the woman let herself down, bent down and picked up her clothes and, without looking at anyone, mumbled something like thanks fellas and staggered out, a tiny bit wobbly on her high heels.

Jessica saw the same woman a little later in the dining alcove on her hands and knees while three men took turns at her from the rear. And jumping ahead, in the early hours of the morning, when Jessica was being had from behind by a big happy man, the same woman put her head in the door and spoke. "Will you be long Gary? I'd like to go. I'm quite tired and ready for bed."

Such was the world of experienced swingers, apparently, and for some reason, Jessica thought about that moment a lot over the coming weeks.

When Jessica made it back into the lounge room, there were still many people chatting and drinking and she realised that maybe not all of them were intending to make out with someone. Or maybe they just hadn't found anyone they wanted to be with.

Jessica suddenly thought of the woman in the kaftan, and wondered how she was getting along and headed off in search of her.

Someone had switched off the bright fluorescent kitchen lights and fetched a bedside lamp and stood it on the nearby kitchen bench. It was adequate and a much softer light.

The Bali hair-braided woman was nowhere in sight. Instead, a naked middle-aged woman was laying on the kitchen table with a man between her legs and with her ankles on his shoulders. Three other naked men stood around the table with their cocks waving as she attempted to grab and swallow each one. She was very vocal and appeared a little out of control, begging for the men to fuck her non stop while at the same time, chastising them loudly.

"One of you bastards hasn't been around to fuck me this month? When I work out which one it is, you'll know about it."

But then Jessica could appreciate the woman's situation and admitted to feeling a little envious.

Jessica moved out and along through the scullery and looked out through the fly wire door to the back garden. There was the kaftan lady, bent double and swaying gently and totally naked under a full moon; and her suitors where many and not exactly who Jessica would have expected. Jessica counted six men with their cocks at the ready but there were also four women amongst them, brandishing what looked like giant dildos attached to their waists with a complex harness.

There seemed to be an already understood pattern of behaviour and Jessica was fascinated.

A woman stood in front of Dunya and told her to stand up straight. Then the woman stepped forward and fed her dildo up into the big woman's vagina. Then another woman would step up behind Dunya and feed a similar dildo in between her huge buttocks. Then men would take it in turns to step forward and shag the two dildo brandishing woman from the rear, the mens movement adding heft, helping push the oversized dildo's into Dunya's enormous vagina and arse.

As the men stood around waiting for their turn, two other women would move amongst them feeling and sucking their cocks to get them hard ahead of their turn with the women and laughingly letting the men handle their heavy sagging dildos.

While Jessica found this interesting, she wasn't sure what was really going on. It wasn't until she was talking to Angela's new friend Sally, in the early hours of the morning after the woman, along with Angela, hunted her down and took her to a little spare bed in the laundry, and smothered Jessica with kisses and wet stuff and took turns heaving themselves joyously into Jessica's vagina and bottom with their dildos, that all was made clear.

Jessica surrendered happily to the honeypot from number 49 and said she'd come over again and spend time with just the two of them.

"Dunya loves men but because of her size they are just not big enough to give her what she wants. She happily lets men suck and play with her tits, but she won't let them fuck her. And even though men can use a dildo, Dunya's preference is for a woman to do her. She says they know better what to do and anyway, she loves their female energy.

"Everyone appreciates her predicament and makes a point of giving her what she wants. Doing things this way means that the women can also get all the cocks they want, at the same time."

Mystery solved. But there was more.

"You might or might not have noticed the size of the dildo's. Dunya bought them online from a sex toy firm in London. Apparently they have quite a range including Draft horses and, would you believe, Unicorns.

"The draft horse dildo's were supposedly from original stud farm castings and came complete with the horses name and providence. It's true. She showed them to me on the internet."

THIRTEEN
POPPY'S PARLOR

Jessica was again visiting her friends, Angela and Craig at their apartment at The Willows retirement village.

They had organised a second swingers party following the success of the one a couple of months earlier, and Jessica was excited when Angela called and invited her.

She began her visit with a passionate moment with her hosts then wandered off, leaving Angela and the newly arrived neighbour, Sally, planning an erotic adventure.

As she was passing by the double doors that led to the little dining area and sun room, she glanced in and saw three men sitting on a sofa. They looked much older than the other men she'd seen so far. They were happily laughing and talking and Jessica thought how relaxed they were and she wanted to know more about them.

"Hello gentlemen. Can I join you?" she ventured as she came close and they looked up at her.

Jessica put them all in their late seventies and thought how she had never seen three men this age together before. They seemed so relaxed and unthreatening and she wanted to know them better.

Three sets of appreciative and smiling eyes stared at Jessica.

"Welcome to the gang of three, dearest lady. You are very beautiful.

Please come and sit with us. Move up Henry and let the girl have a seat. That is Colin up that end, Henry in the middle and I'm John. What is your name?"

"I'm Jessica. Pleased to meet you all."

Jessica squeezed in between Henry and John.

"How is it that three fine looking men like you are all alone. Have you finished with all the lovely woman here already? Or have you been told to behave yourselves?"

The three men laughed and John answered. "Well, Jessica. We are all in our mid eighties but we have one other thing in common. All three of us have wives who are much younger than us and as you can imagine, because of our age, the girls are missing out on some of the things we were once keen to share with them. As a result, we like to bring them somewhere where they can meet younger men and get a stiff bit of you-know-what. This means that we can all stay happily married."

Then Colin added his voice to the conversation. "We can get them up but they're just not hard enough anymore, are they boys?

"We love our wives so we are happy that they can get a good stiff cock in them at do's like this. My Mary came past a few minutes ago to see if we were okay and said all three were having a great time and their only worry was that they might be running out of cocks."

John laughed and said how if that was the case, his Maureen would want him to put on the dildo when they got home and he wouldn't get to sleep until the early hours.

Jessica was fascinated by what these jolly men were saying. She wondered if the three men's wives gave their cocks any attention but decided not to ask.

Jessica decided to play the innocent girl. Well, sort of innocent. She told the three gentlemen about how difficult it was to find men who would just give her a gently touch up and play with her breasts and caress her and talk to her. As she did so, she put a hand on John and Henry's knees and lightly rubbed them.

"That sounds about all we can do, girl. Would you like us to play with you then? We certainly won't hurt you. Why don't you lay yourself across our legs so that we can all have a bit of you. Do that and we'll see how we go. What do you think fella's.

A thrill ran through Jessica's body. She stood up and surveyed the men, then she lifted the hem of her skirt and asked them if she should she lay face up or face down. Two out of three said face down, so the excited girl carefully laid on top of six legs, her heeled sandals touching the arm of the sofa at one end her head on John's trousers at the other end.

"That is nice, isn't it fellas? She's quite something isn't she? Look at those legs."

Jessica felt six sets of fingers moving gently up and down on the back of her legs.

"I bet she's got a nice little bum up here somewhere, too."

Jessica felt someone unzipping her skirt and she lifted herself a little bit and put her hand underneath to show them and help whoever it was, wanting to pull the skirt down.

"May as well take it right off, Col."

With her skirt gone, Jessica felt hands on her bottom.

"Take her knickers off, too, Col."

Jessica rejoiced, knowing three sets of eyes were feasting on her bare bottom. Then she felt a finger on her little anus, going round and round but not intruding.

"Nice little Poppy's parlour", came the voice of Henry.

"How come you call it that, Henry. Never heard it before."

Jessica felt wonderful. Fingers played gently with her ankles and moved her shoes on and off her feet. She wondered if Collin at the end, had a foot or shoe fetish and when he alternated between her two feet, she figured that he had both. She loved it.

"When I was a youngster living in a village in England, the youngest of the girls who lived a couple of doors up from us was named Poppy. You don't hear the name these days. I quite liked it and I liked her.

She was a happy girl but some folk thought she wasn't all there, so to speak. She seemed vague at times and you could never be sure what she was thinking or what she would do next. She wasn't subnormal or anything, though some called her one of gods Angels which in those days usually meant mentally handicapped."

Jessica felt John's hands slide under the top of her body and slide beneath her blouse and find her nipples. This was bliss, she thought.

"When I was much older, my mother told me that Poppy's mum, Ivy Gateshead, told my mum something she had told her daughter when she was fourteen.

"She told the young Poppy that as she got older, men would start to give her a lot of attention and that she had to be especially careful what she did with men or they might get her pregnant. She told her that what she had between her legs was called the bedroom, and what she had between the cheeks of her bum was called the parlour. She went on to tell Poppy that she must never let any boy put his willy in her bedroom, and she should only let him into the parlour, just like when they had special visitors at home.

"She told her that one day, when Poppy had a husband, she could let him into the bedroom so that they would be able to make babies and have a family."

Jessica thought what a lovely story this was and with all the attention her body was getting from the three mens fingers, she felt that she would happily be the mens Poppy and let any of them into her parlour.

"Poppy developed early and her breasts attracted a lot of attention which excited her. Being so innocent and not wanting to offend, she discovered that by letting boys, and later, men into her parlour, she was suddenly much admired and loved by all. She also discovered that she really liked having someone visit in the parlour and it wasn't long before Poppy's parlour was a euphemism in the village for any girls back entrance.

"As she got older and word of Poppy's welcoming parlour spread, there was a constant stream of males seeking her attention and she gave it to them most willingly."

Jessica was loving this story so much. Then she noticed movement beneath her. It was in John's trousers. He was obviously aroused and she couldn't be sure if it was a reaction to touching her or to his story. She figured it was both.

"What a great story, John. I take it you made visits to the parlour?"

"I did Henry. I was a bit younger than Poppy, but when I was around eighteen and she was probably a year or two older, I was out walking near the Oak forest just a mile from the village, with my friend, Bernard, when we ran into Polly. She smiled her dreamy far-away-look smile at us then she said she wanted to show us something.

"Poppy led us off the track into the woods a short distance. Then she turned and unbuttoned our trousers and took out our cocks. She stared at each one lovingly and smiled her dream-like smile and then she took turns, rubbing and sucking them.

"This was all new to us and very exciting. Then she pulled up her skirt and pulled down her knickers and knelt down on the soft leaves, displaying her bottom and asked us to rub our hands over it. Then she said that we had to take turns in putting our cocks into her parlour. She pulled the cheeks of her bum apart and showed us where to put them.

"After a bit of confusion and with Poppy's help, we managed to get into her and happily rode the lady, listening to her moan and groan as though she was unhappy. When we enquired after her wellbeing she informed us that she was very happy and just as long as we were happy, to keep taking turns in her parlour.

"It was a memorable day. Poppy kept us at it until almost dusk, than she stood up and thanked us and disappeared into the forest.

"Over the years Poppy got quite a reputation and there came a time when there was hardly a man in the village, young or old, who hadn't visited Polly's parlour.

"Then one day she met a young man and they fell in love and got married and she went on to give birth to eight beautiful children.

"I was in my twenties and I accompanied my mother too the wedding. I will always remember mum dabbing her eyes as we watched the bride and groom leave the church, and mum saying, 'She's the only girl in the village that deserves to wear white.'"

Jessica could feel the large bump in Johns trousers getting bigger which excited her, and she began to unbutton his fly. She soon discovered his respectable cock and took hold of it and shortly after that, she welcomed it into her mouth.

With a spare hand, she reached down to where Henry also had a lump in his trousers and Jessica signalled to him that she wanted him to expose his member. Then she rubbed her knee against Colin's crotch and felt movement in his trousers.

Jessica swung herself off the men and kneeled on the floor, sucking John and rubbing Henry. Then Jessica moved to suck Henry leaving both hands free to rub Colin's newly liberated cock while continuing to rub John's.

"By jove, this girl has got what it takes. I think I'm actually going to be able to give her something."

John was about to erupt and Jessica managed to get him in her mouth the moment before it happened.

Just as she was swallowing John's present, Henry began to tremble in that way Jessica knew pre-empted a man's orgasm and she managed to get his contribution without loosing a drop.

As the first two men slumped back and smiled through dreamy eyes at their beautiful liberator, Colin spurted forth into Jessica's waiting mouth, then slumped backward alongside the other two.

"What an amazing woman you are, Jessica. I'm sure I can speak for all of us when I say thank you and extend to you our very best wishes," said John, affectionately.

Jessica stood and looked down upon them, regretting it was all over. She felt she could have let them touch and play with her forever.

"Thank you gentlemen. I really enjoyed your company.

"Can a girl be a bit forward and ask if you would like to see me again and if so, where might I find you all? I would love to get your attention again and I would be happy to be your Poppy and let you visit her parlour, and now, thanks to the contraceptive pill, she could even let you into the bedroom.

"I just love being with you any which way. And sucking you all was a bonus. Are you ever available? Unfortunately I'm at work during the day so it would have to be in the evenings or at the weekends."

The men rallied themselves and looked at each other and nodded. Then John sat up and spoke.

"Our wives go to the swingers club together on the second Monday night of each month. They get home very late. At around 1 or 2 am, usually. We three usually get together for a drink and supper and watch TV or play cards.

"I believe I can safely say that we would much prefer to watch and play with you, Jessica. You could come over after eight o'clock to 89 Seaview Crescent, The Willows. We would love to see you."

FOURTEEN

TEGAN'S STORY

Tegan's story was quite different to Leanne 's. Her first sexual experience wasn't really a physical experience, it was simply a voyeuristic
adventure, spying on her promiscuous aunt while on holidays, just
days before Tegan discovered that she too had her very own special
condition.

Tegan missed a few years while she was finishing secondary school
but then returned to the farm one summer for her nineteenth birthday.

Visiting her uncle and aunt on their large sheep property for these
summer holidays was always going to be an adventure. But it wasn't
just the opportunity to ride horses or the farm quad bike.

She had arranged to help her uncle on a neighbouring farm but at
the last minute, just as she was about to get into the utility, her period
arrived and she knew that she should stay home. She apologised to
uncle Bill who kindly agreed that she would be better off staying at the
farm.

Aunt Stacy looked at her intently when Tegan told her what had
happened, and she demanded that Tegan stay in bed all day and said
that she would bring her food to her.

Around mid-day, Tegan's aunt brought a tray of goodies and told her that she mustn't leave the room and that she would check on her again later in the afternoon.

Tegan couldn't help but notice that aunt Stacy seemed different and she was dressed up a little more than usual and that unusually, she was wearing perfume. Tegan knew that other than her trip to the shearing shed with lunches for the shearers and workers in the shed, she wouldn't be leaving the property. So why was her aunt dressed up?

When Tegan heard unfamiliar steps on the kitchen linoleum and the backdoor closing, and she looked out of the window, she saw Stacy carrying two baskets of food and heading towards the shearing shed. And she was amazed to see that her aunt was now wearing high heels. What on earth did that mean?

Tegan decided that being in bed wasn't where she wanted to be.

Tegan dressed and wandered over to the big corrugated iron sheds. The machinery was now silent as the workers had stopped for lunch.

Tegan didn't want to be seen by her aunt as she had promised to stay in bed, so she entered the shed from a little used side door which led into a tiny room which was accessed from where all the full wool bales were stored.

She was about to go into the wool store when she heard a voice from the nearby kitchen area.

"Hello Andrew, you lovely young man. You're my first, darling. Are you excited? Are you pleased to see me? Do you like what you see?"

Tegan watched as the good looking shearer smiled and said he was excited.

"You lovely young man. Now, do you want to pop in from the back or the front?"

"Back please."

Tegan was shocked and mystified with what her aunt was saying and who she was saying it to. Instead of opening the door, she looked through a small round window in the wall beside the door.

Tegan was shocked to see aunt Stacy laying over what looked like a settee or a day bed. She was not wearing knickers and was naked except for her bra and stockings and high heels and Tegan could see a wisp of brown pubic hair just visible between the top of her long stockinged legs. She held her knickers in her hand and her sizeable and shapely backside was pushed out to encourage her visitor.

Tegan drew a shocked breath of surprise as she looked at the fit looking young Andrew standing behind Stacy, holding a large cock, readying himself to enjoy her exciting offering.

Tegan was amazed and excited. She watched, mesmerised as the well built young man pushed his cock so easily into her aunt's vagina. It all happened so effortlessly and Stacy moved her backside around, showing Andrew how she appreciated his efforts.

"Oh yes, Andrew, that is exactly what a girl needs. Keep pushing, darling.

But then, a few moments later, the young man yelled and Stacy yelled "Yes, oh yes." Then the satiated young Andrew disappeared and another man came through the door.

"Robert? You lovely young man. Now it's your turn darling. Show my your cock, sweetheart. Now do you want me from the back or the front? I'll enjoy you whichever way."

"The front please Stacy."

Stacey laid back with her legs apart and pushed her wispy little bush upwards towards an obviously eager Robert. The man quickly put his big and rigid cock into the Stacey's waiting and already saturated vagina.

"Oh yes, Robert. Give it to me you gorgeous man. As hard as you like."

Robert willingly did as he was asked and Tegan was now touching herself between her legs despite the presence of her period.

Another "Yes, yes", and a "more please," and then Robert exploded and was done and on his way.

Tegan watched as her aunt rose and wiped herself with her knickers and rubbed herself vigorously then arched her back and orgasmed and gasped. Then she turned to greet the next man.

"Harry! Looking as hungry for it as ever. How's your hip?"

An older man limped up to Stacy and took her hand in his.

"What will it be, Harry. Anything you like. Is it easier if I suck you off?"

Harry wobbled a bit. He was the permanent shed rouse-about and Tegan knew him because he'd been at the farm for years.

"Cow girl would be good, Stacy, same as before. Make sure you let your tits out and you let them hang in my face. I do love that."

Tegan watched, breathlessly as her aunt first dropped Harry's trousers then helped him remove them. Then she helped him down onto the floor.

"I don't get to do this very often, Harry. Just tell me if I'm not fast enough or if I'm too fast. I'll enjoy myself whichever way. Now first, let's have a suck of this and get it ready."

Stacy was soon riding Harry's upright prick. Then she stopped long enough to reach back and undo her her bra and let her large breasts hang loose. Then she leant forward until her nipples touched Harry's mouth.

"Now suck and bite them like you always do, Harry. You know how I love it."

Tegan was beside herself and only slowly getting over the initial shock of her aunts behaviour.

Then Tegan recalled a conversation between her mother and her sister one night when Tegan was much younger. Although she had no idea what they were talking about, she did remember a few words of what was said.

"It has always been there in the family, darling. Only in the girls, of course. It's a condition that we shouldn't bother trying to fight. Enjoy it! How could you not want to? It's fabulous while it lasts."

When Tegan again focused on what was happening through peeping window in the door, a huge shearer had just arrived and he had already been welcomed by aunt Stacy.

"Suck me off, please Stacey. It was really good last time."

Stacy turned the man and leant him back against the fridge. Then she dropped to her knees and in just a few moments she had two hands holding the biggest cock Tegan had ever seen. Not that Tegan had seen many at that point.

"This is the mouth filler I've been waiting for, George."

Then Tegan watched as her aunt played George's cock like the virtuoso cock sucker that she appeared to be, slurping, licking, deep-throating and tugging, and all the while fingering his huge spunk-filled balls.

Every so often, Stacy would stop and look up at him lovingly, not wanting to put him over the top too quickly.

"I hope you are ready, George. I want all of it down my throat, big man. Don't hold back. Those sluts in the wool sorting room will have to wait and get their share tomorrow. Today, it's all mine. Okay?"

George started to groan and Stacy increased her efforts and suddenly she let out a muffled scream and lifted her head, swallowing like she was drinking from a bottle.

George straightened up and tucked himself back into his trousers.

"Thanks, Luv!"

Tegan watched her aunt sit back, her mouth moving as she savoured George's cum.

Another man arrived.

"Hello Clive. Lovely to see you. And yes I do remember that special something that you like, and to tell you the truth Clive, I like it now much more than I did last time. Is that what you would like?"

Tegan was intrigued. What was this special something?

Tegan watched as Stacy knelt on a chair and bent forward, reaching for a tube of something. Then she put the tube behind her and squirted it in between her buttocks.

"My bottom is ready, Clive. Just do it slowly to start with, dear man, then you can get stuck into me. I will love it.

"And don't forget. You can shag all the girls in the bum like this, Clive. You don't want to get them pregnant do you. Doing it like this when you are having the sweet things up against the dance hall wall at the next Bachelor and Spinster Ball means you won't have to worry about babies and nor will they."

Tegan was amazed to see her aunt's large and attractive bum being so energetically fucked. And what is more, Stacy was loving it, seemingly as much as was the well endowed and lucky Clive.

"I think I'm going to want to do this more often, Clive. I'll put it on my list of things on offer. That will be fun.

"Now, squirt inside me, Clive. I want to feel an anal explosion."

Tegan was now imagining that what her aunt was enjoying was happening to her and she was very excited.

And as an alternative place to put a cock to avoid pregnancy, well that was just the best news ever.

Tegan came at the same time as Clive and Stacy but managed to do it silently. Then she tottered off back to the house and her bedroom where she lay exhausted and exhilarated and totally mind-blown at what she had seen and heard.

But of course, the burning question now uppermost in her mind couldn't help but be about whether or not she would or had inherited the same mysterious condition as her mother and her aunt. And should she be worried?

As Tegan fingered herself, she remembered in graphic detail all of the men she had just watched fucking aunt Stacy and visualising what each one did. Then she found herself murmuring "Oh yes, yes?" Then Tegan thrust her pussy upwards and orgasmed and whispered, "Oh yes, dear aunty. You beautiful lucky sexy bitch!"

FIFTEEN

TEGAN AND UNCLE BILL

It was a week after the wool shed incident and Tegan had agreed to accompany her uncle Bill on his second visit to a large neighbouring property to help sort cattle. Bill had studied agriculture and had a degree in animal reproduction and advised most of his neighbours on their stock breeding program.

Her uncle had arranged for them to be away for three nights.

This week, more yearlings were to be separated from their dams and the older cows moved to new pasture to prepare for mating while those rejected would be fattened for market. Breeders and heifers would be sorted according to Bill's guidelines.

Bill was looking forward not just to the work, but to also being with his late friend's wife, Mavis.

His friend, James, had died in a truck collision on the Cobb highway four years earlier.

Bill and he and James's wife were very close, sufficiently so that James and Mavis were fully aware of Bill's situation at home and his wife's occasional bouts of promiscuity. Both respected Bill's commitment to Stacy and never asked questions.

James had always said that if anything ever happened to him, he would want Bill to look after Mavis. "She's got a soft spot for you Bill so don't let me down."

It was a good two years after James died that Bill was visiting the farm. He always camped in the shearers quarters but shared an evening meal with Mavis and her two boys, Jimmy and Maurice. The boys were great workers and loved working with Bill when he visited.

The two young men sometimes joked when they were working with Bill out in the cattle yards.

"Dad reckoned you would be the only bloke who could handle mum if anything ever happened to him. We think dad meant it. She gets lonely, Bill. Us two think you should be worried about her. She needs something."

And so it came to pass, that one day when Bill was working at their farm and the boys were away doing a course and Bill joined Mavis for dinner, the good looking woman fixed Bill with a special look.

"I'm not getting any younger Bill, but I'm still young enough. I think it is time you took me to bed. I know James would approve."

Bill was transfixed by the smile he'd grown to love. It was aimed at him and it wasn't going to let him go.

Bill put down his knife and fork, wiped his mouth with his serviette and stood up. As Mavis watched in awe, Bill came around the table and, taking her hand lifted her up. Then he led her to the bed in the room nearby and turned her and bent her over and lifted her skirt.

"Oh my God, what's got into you Bill. I didn't mean that you had to …"

Bill pulled down Mavis's knickers and parted Mavis's thighs and stared at her delicious backside. Then he affectionately rubbed her vagina. Then he unzipped himself and effortlessly slid his cock into her already very wet and slippery cunt until it was firmly lodged in a place he'd so often thought about.

"Oh Bill, Yes! Yes, you darling man. Do whatever you want to me. Lets make up for lost time. Fuck me, please. Fuck me stupid, you adorable man! Do it to me darling!"

When the two had cleared the dishes and Mavis had taken his arm and led him to her bedroom, the two couldn't stop kissing and Mavis couldn't stop holding and rubbing Bill's cock.

Throughout the night Mavis would wake up and suck Bill's cock and he would roll on top of her and shag her slowly while she sobbed and pushed her fingernails into his shoulders. Then he would roll her to be on top of him and she would laugh and ride him, calling out yes, yes as she rediscovered her sexuality. This was a turning point for both of them.

Tegan was feeling more than just healthy. She couldn't put her finger on it, but she just felt fantastic and was looking forward to time away with her uncle.

During the week she had pondered the question of the so called condition that her mother had spoken of and what Tegan had now seen, was strong evidence of it in her aunts behaviour.

One question which wouldn't go away was about her father, James and about uncle Bill. What would be their take on what happened to their wives on those occasions when the condition manifested itself. How did they cope? Did this have something to do with her parents separation?

Bill and Tegan had set out earlier than usual as the weather for the day was uncertain and Bill didn't want to be caught on wet dirt roads, not that it was really a problem other than slowing them down.

Sitting beside uncle Bill in the old land cruiser was fun as was getting away to a different place. Tegan felt excited but different but she couldn't work out what she was feeling or what was causing it.

After about a half hour, Tegan asked her uncle if he wouldn't mind pulling over onto a side track behind some trees so that she could have a pee. He happily did so and Tegan hopped out and disappeared behind some bushes.

It was while Tegan had her knickers down and having a pee that the world suddenly seemed more simple to her. She suddenly felt freer than she ever had before. She removed her knickers and threw them away, not stopping to wonder why she had done so. Then she went and got back into the truck.

"All good?" Asked Bill

"Fantastic, thanks dear Uncle," she laughed and the two made eye contact. But then Bill suddenly went quiet and just stared at Tegan.

"What is it, you sexy man?" Tegan inquired with a big smile, unsure why she'd used the word sexy.

Bill continued staring.

"You've got that look, Tegan. The look your mother and aunt have when their condition takes over. Are you all right sweetheart? Not feeling strange?"

Tegan stared back with her new smile, conscious that she was feeling different but uncertain what that feeling was. Her uncle was looking at her in a funny way. She noticed how handsome he was. Then she blurted out a sentence that came from somewhere deep in the recesses of her dormant mind.

"I want to suck your cock, uncle Bill. Please let me!"

As Tegan spoke she reached across and felt the front of her uncle's jeans. Then without hesitation she began to unbuckle his belt and when that was done, she opened his zipper.

Uncle Bill was no stranger to this condition and he was wise enough to not try and change the course of events.

It had been explained to him by a specialist who likened the condition to sleep-walking. Just as you should not try to wake up a sleep-walker, you should not try to make your wife see things differently while in that semi-dream state.

His experience with his wife and also with Tegan's mother, Louise, many years ago had taught him much.

When Louise and Stacy suddenly succumbed to their conditions at the same time, triggered by a boisterous party night, he and Tegan's father had been forced to swap wives just to keep them from running amuck. Even then, there were incidents on that night involving a visiting football team.

Tegan's father and mother had eventually parted even though they both loved each other dearly.

Bill and Stacy stayed together, probably because Bill understood the problem a little better and accepted Stacy for who she was regardless of the condition. He knew all about her visits to the shearers and shed hands and most times kept away to avoid any unpleasantness or confusion.

Now he was confronted with a younger version and he was trying not be worried by it.

———————

Tegan lowered her mouth onto her first cock and her world changed. She slowly took Bill in her hand and ran the tips of her fingers along its length. Ecstasy was the feeling running around in her head and her body.

The two sat in the truck while Tegan had her way with her uncle. Then while she looked up at him with that extraordinary smile that he understood so well, she unfastened and pulled down her jeans and in a confident voice said, "You can play with my pussy, uncle Bill. I'm not yet on the pill so I'm sorry but you can't fuck me.

By this time, Bill was finding it difficult to be his rational self.

I think in this situation, Tegan, I would prefer you call me William. I'm not comfortable with the uncle label.

Tegan smiled up at him. "Yes, all right William. I'm fine with that."

"Now I'm thinking that if you put your penis in my bottom hole and you come, I wouldn't get pregnant would I uncle Bill? Sorry, I mean William?"

Bill stared at what was suddenly a sexually precocious young woman and he knew that there was nothing he could do about it. Talking to Tegan rationally wasn't going to get anywhere. In this condition he could only go along with her desires and hopefully settle her down and get her through it all. In the meantime, the fact that she was enjoying herself wasn't lost on him.

Bill lent over and fiddled in the glove box, retrieving a tube of hand cream which he handed to Tegan.

"Grab that blanket off the back seat and take it behind those bushes and take off your jeans, Tegan. I'll fuck your bottom. If it's your first time, it might be a bit uncomfortable. But the sooner you get to like it, the more you will be able to enjoy yourself without worrying about babies. Okay?"

Tegan's eyes shone brightly. "Oh yes, William, lets do that. Thank you so much."

An excited Tegan was already kneeling on the blanket when Bill arrived behind the bushes, her neat little bum pushed upwards and waiting like a flower waiting to attract a passing bee.

Bill put his cock between Tegan's tiny buttocks and found the spot she had just lubricated. Then he moved it forward, spreading her buttocks apart with his hands.

"Oh, William. I love you doing this. Even if we don't get it right today, promise me we'll try again soon?"

Bill promised, staring at the delightful vision in front of him.

Bill pushed his cock gently into Tegan's tiny anus, not confident that he would make an entry. But then magic happened and suddenly the head of his penis was inside Tegan and Bill wanted to push on.

"Are you okay, Tegan?"

"Yes, William. It feels so very nice. Do it some more, please."

To Bill's surprise, it wasn't long before he found his belly right up tight against the girls buttocks. He felt that she was fully impaled on the end of his big cock and couldn't understand why she wasn't complaining.

"Are you still okay, Tegan?"

There was silence, then a little voice wafted back to him.

"I'm in heaven, William. Do whatever you need to do to come in me. I'm not letting you go until you've done me properly. I want to feel what its like when you come."

Bill set about enjoying himself and it wasn't long before his body stiffened and he erupted. Then the little voice spoke again.

"Oh, William! That was so beautiful. Promise you will do it to me again, soon? Please, William?"

Bill promised he would but then told Tegan to get herself together so that they could finish the trip and get on with the job.

Tegan looked for and found the knickers she had thrown away and she put them on. For the rest of the trip, she felt stuff running out of her and she celebrated her first anal intercourse. But she knew she wasn't done yet. Her world of sexual excitement was only just starting.

SIXTEEN
ANGIE'S STORY

I had moved to the city at age twenty three to live with Mum's old school friend, Betty. I had worked mainly in education so getting a position in the office of the Events Coordinator at a university was a slight step up and the pay was much better.

One of the Events staff tasks that I particularly enjoyed was going on camps. It meant that I got away from my crazy landlady, whom I loved dearly but who could be quite demanding.

The university owned a couple of holiday camps, one in the mountains the other in bushland that fronted a beautiful beach. I got to know them both very well.

As a member of staff, I was involved in the planning of student activities and insuring that everything ran to plan. This involved getting the students up early and organising them for bush walks or beach trips, or whatever the preplanned itinerary dictated.

Most times everything was good and the students who were mainly in their early to mid twenties were great.

Occasionally there would be a couple who could prove tiresome and shirk their rostered duties, or disrupt some well-planned activity. We tactfully tried to sort these students and put them into roles where they couldn't easily cause problems.

My story begins with a planned combined canoeing and bush-walking trip. Everybody knew what tasks they had been allotted. The weather was perfect, and at nine fifteen we congregated at the centre of the camp, then moved off towards the jetty and the canoes.

It was at that moment that one of the staff noticed that two of the students were missing, and I was sent to find them and hurry them up.

I headed up to the rows of tents. It was very quiet, as everyone had already headed to the beach.

I approached the tent of the two missing students, Ray and Kevin. As I drew close I thought I heard a sound. I walked around to the back of their tent and peeped through the mosquito netting of the small back window.

Ray and Kevin were laying stark naked on the floor. Each had a hand on the other's stiff cock and both were rubbing and tugging furiously. It was so exciting. I'd seen girls playing with each other but never boys. Instead of immediately leaving, I stood fascinated and watched while rubbing myself between my legs. Then the two ejaculated and I watched in awe as their cum squirted up over their belly and chest. Then I quietly left, my emotions swirling and my pussy dripping.

I reported back that the two couldn't be found and they were both marked down for onerous camp duties.

The thirty or more students on the trip had a great time. It was interesting observing them. Some seemed so young while others were enjoying adulthood. All were entertaining and often I smiled watching what they were up to.

One girl, Judy Somerville, was the girl who had everything going for her and commanded attention wherever she went. Not only was she tall and shapely, she was also beautiful to look at and spoke confidently on all matters.

If Judy Somerville had a problem, it must surely have been that she was what some boys would call a "cock tease". She knew that she reigned supreme over all the other girls in her year and that she was probably the most desired female on the campus. And if that wasn't enough, she had a more than adequate bosom, about which the boys could never pass up the opportunity to make a comment.

One wanted to feel sympathetic to Judy, but it just was not possible.

Judy had a couple of girlfriends but they were only there to bathe in her glory and enjoy her occasional largesse as a wealthy benefactor. Judy Somerville's parents were well-to-do, and she made sure that everyone knew about it.

She had a boyfriend who sometimes picked her up from university in his father's expensive European sports car.

A month or more after this camping event and after work one day, I called out to our school camp naughty boys, Ray and Kevin, as they headed off for the Mall. I still had a vivid memory of them rubbing each others cocks and it couldn't help but make me feel hot. I was dressed in my tight skirt and heels and I felt more than adequate to impress them.

The two young men came over and I told them that I had a few hours paid work for them at my house. They said that they were interested and I asked them if they could get there as soon as they finished their last tutorial on Friday.

When Kevin, the cheeky one, replied "We are expensive Miss," I replied "So am I, but everything is negotiable. Just be there."

Friday came and the two lads knocked on my door and I showed them in.

I told them to follow me and led them to the lounge and asked them to sit on the sofa. They were slightly out of their comfort zone, and a bit self-conscious.

Male students are not too interested in women's clothing, being usually fixated only on her anatomy. Clothed but preferably naked. I was wearing a very tight and extremely short skirt that accentuated my main asset, a prominent backside, and also a very low cut top. White hold-ups were my stockings of choice and high heels and lots of lipstick were part of my deliberate slutty masquerade.

Hopefully they'd notice that I looked a little different from the way I looked at work.

First, I told them to each move aside and make a space for me on the sofa, as I had something to tell them. I sat down making sure my skirt rose above my knees. Then, on pretence of needing to switch something off in the kitchen, I stood and walked slowly away from them, towards the swing door.

Immediately I passed through the door I turned, and peeped through a crack on the side. Both boys were grinning and nodding, and Kevin made a gesture with his hand indicating he was doing something rude with himself and probably with me.

I smiled to myself. Bingo! They've noticed.

I came back and sat on the sofa.

"Now boys, it's your lucky day."

"How come, Miss?"

"Well, how will I put this? I'm sure you both have fantasies. In fact I'm certain you both fantasise about the lovely Judy Somerville, for instance?"

There was a stunned silence.

"Oh, and in case you are wondering why I invited you, you are here to help me with my fantasies. Yes, girls have fantasies too."

The two stared at me with a wide-eyed look of disbelief.

"And just in case you both feel disinclined to share my fantasy with me, I should tell you one important thing.

"I saw you tugging each others cocks in your tent at camp last month. So if you don't do as I ask, I could put out the rumour that you two are wanking each other, and that probably has something to do with you not being able to get or hang on to a girlfriend."

The two young men stared at me then at each other. Kevin turned to me.

"Oh no Miss, you can't do that. We don't do it much, Miss. Please don't tell anyone."

"Good, Kevin; now, when you were both playing with each others cocks, what was your fantasy at that moment? Ray? You're first.

"Gees Miss, do we really have to do this? This is so embarrassing. We came to work in your shed Miss, we should get started."

"Kevin, you are the cheeky one. Tell me what you were thinking about. Were you thinking about Judy Somerville's gorgeous body? Were you fucking Miss Somerville in your head, while Ray was giving you the hand job?"

Kevin pulled a face.

"That bitch should be fucked. She's such a bitch."

Then Ray added his thoughts.

"Yeah Miss, every bloke at school wants to fuck her. She's so sexy and good-looking."

"So Kevin, if you had Judy Somerville here right now and you could do anything you wanted with her, what would you do? Tell me, Kevin. What is your fantasy about the most desirable Judy? You can say whatever's in your head."

The two boys each looked past me, and at each other and grinned.

"Well, Kevin?"

"I'd first put her over my knee and pull down her knickers and give her big backside a good whack. In fact, I'd push her over the back of this seat, drag down her pants and spank her till her cheeks turned red and she screamed for mercy. That's what I'd do, Miss."

"That sounds very exciting Kevin. Thank you. You're next, Ray. You suddenly have the sexy Judy Somerville in front of you. What would your fantasy be? How would you handle the dear girl? Would you woo her with kind words, or would you have something else in mind? Tell us, Ray."

Big Ray coloured up behind his youthful chin stubble.

"Well, Miss, I'd start by pulling her top off, Miss, then I'd bite and suck her big tits, then I'd pull out my stiffy and make her suck it, Miss."

The two exchanged looks and grinned. Then Kevin spoke.

"Yes, Miss, we would show her what's what."

I eyed the two and notice that at least one had a slight bulge in his pants.

"Now boys, would you like to hear my fantasy? Are you both

ready? Remember, I said you are here to help me."

Both boys were suddenly more forthcoming.

"Yes, Miss, whatever you want, Miss."

"Here we go then. This is *my* fantasy."

Two sets of eyes stared at me and I noticed that one lad had a hand moving awkwardly on his trousers.

"Well I'm not as lucky as Judy in the looks and figure departments so my fantasy is that I am really Judy Somerville, and that I am suddenly trapped alone in this room with the two of you."

As I spoke, I placed a hand on each lad's trouser front and let my fingers search for signs of life. There was an audible gasp from Ray, and Kevin wriggled a little.

"Judy Somerville is getting a little excited, sitting beside two of her most enthusiastic admirers, and she notices that things are happening inside their trousers. She reaches out, unzips each of you and gets out your cocks. Having one in each hand makes Judy very happy, and very horny."

I was unzipping the lads as I spoke. Kevin's cock sprang out of his trousers and I untangled Ray where he was caught up in his underpants.

Suddenly I was holding two exciting lumps of meat and I couldn't believe my luck. Neither of the lads objected.

"Oh Miss? Your fantasy is fantastic. What happens next?"

"Yes, what happens, Miss?"

"Judy is very excited. She has a lovely cock in each hand and she moves her hands gently up and down, just like this."

The cocks in my hands were now very hard.

"Judy Somerville is getting more and more excited until she can stand it no longer, and tears off her top and her bra and exposes her big tits to her admirers."

I let go of the boys at this point and removed my top and bra. Then I closed my hand around their erections once again.

Both lads were red-faced, and stared at my breasts.

"Now Ray, Judy's breasts are all yours. Suck them while she's offering them."

I let go of Ray's cock and put a hand behind his head and pulled him to my chest. He immediately opened his mouth and gorged himself on my nipples, moving rapidly from one breast to the next and back again.

Kevin gazed at what was happening. His jaw was slack and his mouth was open. I let go of him and unzipped my skirt, lifted myself without disturbing my tit sucker and slipped the skirt down and away.

Kevin's eyes bulged. Then I slid myself down on the sofa a little, and lifted my legs in the air.

"Judy wants Kevin to smack her bottom while Ray is sucking on her big titties. Please get down on the floor and make Judy happy, Kevin."

Kevin practically fell off the sofa onto the floor. He knelt and stared in awe at my backside and my stockinged legs and my heeled shoes.

"My fantasy, Kevin, so do as you are told. Take Judy's panties off please. Oh, and when you've got her panties off, Kev, she wants you to grab a handful of her hairy pussy and kiss and lick it. Push your tongue right inside her. She's wanting it desperately."

I really didn't need to say or do a lot more.

The boys where on fire. I was suddenly without a skirt, pants or bra and two gorgeous young men where feeding on me, like crocs on a herd of wildebeests crossing a river, and I lay back to fully enjoy it. I was in "bad boy" land and I was in heaven. Two hungry cocks took turn about in my welcoming vagina.

Occasionally I would ask for a little something like "Judy wants you to play with her tits some more, Kevin darling" or "Judy wants you to suck her clit, Ray."

As I stared at the two big red shiny cocks that had excited me when I first saw them at the camp, I drifted off into a dream world and memories.

I recalled being at the local dance and going outside for some fresh air. I walked around for a few minutes and just as I was thinking of going back inside, I spied Stella Forbes leaning back against the wall and tugging on Denis Fuller's cock.

At that moment, something must have gone wrong and Stella yelled "No," and marched off.

Before I could even think about what I was doing, I moved up behind Denis and quietly spoke. "Can I help you with that, Denis?"

Suddenly I was tossing off a very big hard cock. But then it wasn't just the two of us. Two of Denis's mates appeared and I was being offered two more delicious looking penises. One of the men lifted up my dress and pulled down my knickers and very soon they were taking turns with my more than willing pussy doggy style while I happily continued rubbing the two in front of me.

I was in heaven and I think they were too.

———

"You're doing a fantastic job, boys. Please try not to blow your load yet, though, because Judy will want you to do something else with your cocks soon."

A short time later I judged that moment had arrived.

"Back off boys; Judy wants to turn over."

I moved down and knelt on the floor. The boys held their cocks and watched lustfully.

"Look at her arse and her stockings, she's so beautiful Kev. I've only seen that in porn videos. And much sexier than my aunts."

I interpreted the comment as a compliment and was naturally interested to discover more about Ray's aunt. But that would have to wait.

"Now boys, Judy would like you to slide your lovely cocks into her wet pussy and fuck her. Take it in turns. She can suck one of you while the other is in her slippery cunt."

The boys were good. They had managed (I suspect with great difficulty) to hold on until the moment when Judy told each of them separately to empty their balls in her.

We ended the day with me back on the sofa with a stocking round my ankle and a shoe missing, being gently licked and touched as one of the boys played with the bows on my stocking tops.

I complimented the lads.

"Thank you, Kevin! Thank you, Ray! You have satisfied my fantasy perfectly. And I hope you both enjoyed yourselves."

"Oh yes Miss, you're the best. We loved your fantasy, playing Judy, but it was the real you who was really fantastic, Miss Angie."

I thought I noticed that Kevin had a more sensitive look in his eye and his manner had changed.

"Miss Angie?"

"Yes, Ray?"

"I'm in love with you now. Bugger Judy Somerville."

"Me too!" murmured Kevin.

"Hmm, buggering Miss Judy Somerville? Now that's a fantasy I will definitely think about."

The boys exchanged knowing smiles.

"We would be glad to help in the garage any time, Miss Angie."

That is not quite the end of the story. After some time away on holidays I returned to the school. I hadn't been back more than a day when Kevin and Ray met me outside the university gates.

"Hello, you two. Not getting into too much trouble, I hope?"

They both laughed.

Ray started to talk.

"Miss Angie! We wondered if … ?"

"Come on, spit it out, Ray."

"What he wants to say Miss, is that we would be very happy to help you clean up the garage anytime you feel like it."

I laughed. This seemed vaguely like a proposition, or was "cleaning up the garage" a new euphemism for young university student to describe an orgy?

"Well, boys, I'm not against the idea, but I should tell you that last time my crazy landlady Betty, whom I live with, was away and so I had the house to myself. Now she is back."

A downcast look crossed their faces.

"Mind you, I suspect Betty might be a randy lady. She might love to have some young cock around the house."

Both lads straightened up and smiled.

"Is she as beautiful as you, Miss?"

"In a different way, perhaps. She might be just what you young men need, a mature woman who knows what to do with what you've got in your trousers."

Kevin and Ray laughed heartily.

"I think while I was fantasising about being Judy Somerville, Judy would also enjoy having a mature friend there to take care of one of you while she handles the other one. Do you think your up for a double act, lads?"

"God, yes. Can we really do that, Miss Angie?"

"Leave it with me. I'll check with Betty. In the meantime, you both have a tentative booking for Saturday afternoon at two-thirty.

"Oh yes, and by the way, I think Judy and her friend might enjoy a good buggering, so save yourselves. You'll need all the strength you can muster."

Betty stared at her long and hard when Angie told her what she had done with Ray and Kevin. Then when she said how she had invited the young men to visit her and Betty on Saturday afternoon and she hoped her landlady would be okay with that, Betty screamed her excitement, uncharacteristically grabbing Angie and kissing her on the mouth.

"I'll be ready for them, darling. Now where have I put my ladies' razor?"

It was unfortunate that Angie needed to attend to something at work at the university on Saturday morning. She wasn't going on this particular camping trip, but she was in charge of the organisation details which needed some last minute tweaking.

It took longer for Angie to sort out so she was feeling anxious as she raced to get things finished. At one forty-five Angie raced to the carpark and headed home

The freeway was crowded and she wished she had taken a different route. Then when the traffic suddenly stopped and Angie switched on her radio for news, it was not good. A three-truck pile up quite some distance ahead was the problem. And their were injuries and ambulance were on the way.

Angie could not believe this was happening to her, and when she discovered that she had left her phone at the office and she couldn't get in touch with Betty, she realised that all the organising of their planned erotic dalliance had been for nothing.

Angie panicked when she saw the naked form of Betty propped up against the sofa. Her eyes were shut and she seemed not to be breathing and she was sitting in a pool of something wet. Betty looked so peaceful. Her legs were wide apart and her head lolled forward, her chin resting on her chest. Lipstick was smeared all over her face. Then Betty's eyes opened.

"Hello, darling. Thank you Ange. That was fantastic. They promised they'd come back next week at the same time and give it to me all over again but said they would need to check with you first to see if it was okay. They've only just left.

"They just couldn't stop fucking me, Ange. They mumbled something about Miss Angie being right about me. They said I had a magic cunt. Anyway they each filled it twice. Wonderful!.

"It will be okay, won't it darling? You will invite them back won't you?"

Angie reached down and leisurely pulled on one of Betty's nipples.

"Yes, it will be okay, Betty but perhaps a little later in the day so that I can be sure to get here next time. I don't want to miss out a second time."

Angie reached down further and put two fingers into Betty's wet cunt then put them up to her mouth and licked them.

"They were so good to me. They didn't refuse me a thing I asked for. They seemed to love me sucking their testicles while I rubbed their cocks.

"I had almost forgotten how I used to love wanking the blokes at work.

"There was hardly a day went by when I didn't get my hands on at least two or three as each invited me to check something with them in the stationery cupboard. I always sucked them dry then laughed and told them to explain that to their wives and girlfriends when they got home."

Angie stared down at Betty and suddenly she felt really horny and Betty sensed her need for a touch-up.

"Take your clothes off, darling and come down here and lie on me. I'd love to feel you up, Ange. You're such a sexy, voluptuous slut."

Angie stripped and collapsed on top of her landlady who reached up for Angie's fluffy tuft and guided her face down between her legs. Then she ran her hands over Angie's significant large and beautiful backside and pulled her close.

"Oh God, you feel so good, Angie. You're just a big randy bitch on season, aren't you, darling. Just like me. Lick my cunt, Ange. You know there is something there the boys left. It's very fresh."

The two women rubbed and fondled and humped each other and both took turns screaming and coming until they finally lay still and agreed that they were very hungry.

Angie began to put her clothes on.

"Call for a Thai takeaway, Angie. I'll pay."

"I can't, Betty. I've left my phone at work. Oh, but I can use yours."

"Whatever! And Angie?"

'Yes, my sexy looking landlady?"

"I want you to come into my bed tonight, Ange. I want my head between your delicious thighs. I want you to suffocate me while I recall all the fun I had with the lads today and fantasise about getting it all again next week. Pretty please?"

"Sure thing, darling; just so long as I can get on top of your skinny arse with my little rubber friend and hump it till it glows under the quilt."

"It's a deal."

"Yellow curry or green, Betty? I'm happy with either."

SEVENTEEN

AFTER CHOIR PRACTICE

Jenny had been at an art gallery opening of new works, and sitting with a group of women, some of whom she had never met.

She got on well with a pleasant lady who talked about interesting things, not just the usual boring holiday plans or a forthcoming sea cruise.

Jenny could not remember what led to this particular conversation, but the woman's story went something like this.

The woman (her name was Celia Ashbee) had a son teaching at a university whose friend, teaching in another faculty, had a friend who told him a rude story.

The friend of the friend of the friend said that one of his final year students and some other young men were in a church choir and that they had a great time each week at the church after choir practice, with two very willing women.

Jenny suddenly got very interested at this point, but tried to hide her enthusiasm, not wanting the nice lady to think ill of her.

"Did the friend of the friend of the friend say if the young man described what happened, Celia?"

Celia poured more tea and selected a sandwhich. Jenny estimated that she was perhaps a little older than herself, a well-kept woman in her late forties or early fifties.

Celia continued her story, lowering her voice and looking around furtively as she spoke.

"It seems that the two women, the music teacher and the organist, would wait until everyone had left at the end of practice. A couple of the older lads who were in the know, went and hung around outside in the churchyard and would be joined by half a dozen of their village mates who were not in the choir but definitely in the know.

"Then the two women would go back inside the vestry, change their clothes, putting on stockings and suspenders, high heels and short skirts, along with lots of makeup, then unlock the door and let the boys in."

Jenny found the story fascinating, and erotic.

"My goodness, Celia, stories like this could cause a sudden increase in the sizes of congregations across the land. Please tell me more."

Celia laughed, enjoying her new friend's sense of humour and impressed with Jenny's seeming lack of shockability.

"Did he say what actually happened after the boys entered the vestry?"

Jenny's new friend coloured up and Jenny looked at her appreciatively. Celia, on the one hand a very proper upper middle-class woman of impeccable taste, hid a fun-loving naughty side which one would never have observed except via the subject matter of this conversation.

"He did, Jenny. He did indeed. He said that in a very small anteroom there was a mattress covered with a bedspread, probably an emergency bed in case someone in the congregation suddenly took poorly.

"He said that the two women knelt on the mattress and called to the boys to come in, in pairs. Then they told the boys to show them what they had in their trousers. Once they were on display, each woman would put a lads penis in her mouth and suck it; then after a while they would look up at the young man's face and say …"

By this time, Jenny was mesmerised by Celia's story and, it should be said, by the delightful Celia. Her looks, her beautiful voice, her smile, even the lines on her face spoke of intelligence and joy and

Jenny suspected, passion as well. Her fine clothes spoke of finer garments beneath, a satin camisole perhaps, expensive serviceable panties with just a touch of lace? And was she a woman who preferred wearing stockings or did she choose tights?

"Say it, Celia. Tell me what she said. You are committing story interruptus. Please, don't leave me hanging."

Celia burst out laughing, then put her hand over her mouth and looked around like a naughty girl. Then she leant closer to Jenny and reached her hand out and placed it on Jenny's knee and fondled it, and whispered.

"Suck or fuck?"

Jenny stared at Celia's sparkling eyes, bright with mirth.

"Gosh Celia, we're getting to the high notes now."

"Then, if the boy replied with the 'f' word, the woman immediately does an about face, showing her rear end and, it is said, not wearing any knickers, at which point the young fellow had his way.

"If he has any difficulty finding his way, and if the woman beside her is facing the front and has a moment with a free hand, she will lean across and put him in. If not, a hand will come through the woman's legs to grab him and sort him out."

Celia stopped talking and stared at Jenny. She looked flushed and excited. She was fascinated with Jenny and for a moment bore the look of a lover. She loved Jenny's relaxed unfazed way of seeing things.

Jenny looked back at her, lovingly.

There was suddenly a hush as people prepared for a final concert piece by three young violinists.

"Celia?"

"Yes, Jenny?"

"Can I write down my telephone number and give it to you? And maybe we could catch up some time soon. I love talking to you, so I hope we can see each other again."

"Please, yes. And I will call you very soon. You are great company and I do get lonely for someone to talk with who is happy to talk about all sorts of things."

Jenny stared lovingly at Celia and was pleasantly surprised when the beautiful woman's hand wandered a little further along Jenny's knee. And Jenny was certain Celia left her hand there for longer than one would expect.

Celia stared back at Jenny, then in a little voice, murmured, "I do get lonely, Jenny. Maybe you could help fix that. I would so love it if you did."

Jenny put her hand under the hem of her skirt and joined her fingers with Celia's. Then she moved the fingers gently up between her thighs and made little circles with them on her stocking tops. Celia gasped and then sighed.

"I will really enjoy trying, Celia. Be warned though! I'm already excited. A beautiful woman like yourself could easily trigger my animal passion and the consequences might be serious."

Celia coloured up and covered her mouth with her hand.

"Can I take that as a promise of things to look forward too, Jenny? Please tell me it is."

Celia let go of Jenny's fingers and moved her hand much further up her leg, pushing two fingers under a suspender and stroking the bare flesh and Jenny knew that Celia was indeed propositioning her and was overjoyed.

"Oh yes, Celia, we will visit heaven together, I'm sure.

———

Three violins started to tune-up. Two hands squeezed momentarily and appreciative smiles were exchanged.

Two woman had discovered one another and for them, the world offered a promise of excitement and love.

EIGHTEEN

MAUDE AND HER FRIEND

Maude was pleased to see her best friend Gwen. They had known each other from school days and their every adolescent adventure had been shared.

"I thought you might like to do something a bit different around midday on Wednesday Gwen. I know you enjoyed it last time. At least I think you did?"

Gwen had just finished checking her messages on her phone and looked up

"Why do you think I came up so quickly from Melbourne darling? How could I not want to go out and do that special thing that we enjoyed last time. In fact I even packed a little number so that I could better compete with you. Anyway! I'm only sucking from the window this time."

Maude let out a raucous laugh. "You said that last time, darling, and in less than ten minutes you were out of the car minus your knickers and kneeling on your blanket and with your rear end in the air, advertising your crown jewels to the world. There were three blokes lined up, all ready to have you."

"It was five, actually."

"I was a tiny bit busy myself, Gwen, so forgive me for not counting them accurately."

"They were all such gentlemen. They all asked if it was okay if they came inside me; lovely men. I told them I enjoyed a cream pie at any time and to be my guest."

Maude laughed. "I hadn't realised you liked it that much. In fact there was a moment when I was worried that you were overdoing it. That last chap was certainly into you in a big way. I was worried he might hurt you."

"No, Maude! I was screaming because I was loving it. He just did it for me, especially when he stood me up and laid me over the front of the car.

"He certainly knew what to do with his penis. Fast then slow then intermittent, a bit hard on the right side then straight up the middle. He was wonderful. I came three times. I wonder if I can find him again."

"Well, I was in fear of the two of you denting the bonnet of the Merc. I was almost ready to ask him for his address and phone number in case there was damage."

Gwen couldn't stop laughing.

"I wish you had, Maude. Then I could call him up and ask for a repeat performance."

Maude and her husband Gareth were members of the exclusive Eros Vally Golf Club. It covered a large area and nestled in between the foot of Mount Eros and the Pacific Ocean. Areas of woodland were scattered across the course and shady and often isolated parking areas could be discovered off of the regular tracks.

Eros Vally Golf Club was different to any other club. It had a huge membership but mysteriously, only a small number of golfing enthusiasts, the reason being because the Club was renowned for one feature only; Dogging.

Most of this activity happened after 9pm on a Friday night, although lunchtime on a Wednesday was quite popular with bored housewives on fine winter days.

People, particularly women, regularly wore attractive masquerade masks to hide their identity and a mask also helped to hide any unflattering signs of ageing.

There were other ways of achieving a level of anonymity, Neatly fitted covers for the number plates was one and old duvet's thrown across the bonnet of a car served the dual purpose of hiding the car while adding a degree of comfort to those enjoying themselves over the front of the car.

And no one called each other by their real name.

None of this mattered in the end. If they wanted to, people would eventually work out who you were. It was more a form of genteel protocol intended to shield your identity from who you were interacting with.

Maude and Gareth enjoyed what was once termed an open marriage. Both enjoyed their daily lives unencumbered by each ones dalliances.

Gareth knew that Maude knew the hot details relating to his early morning exercise regime. This included running around centennial park with Aline, their stunningly beautiful next-door neighbour and wife of the eccentric and likeable, Harry.

The beautiful Brazilian trophy wife was also a close friend of Maude and confided in her every detail of her life when Aline visited most mornings for coffee and gluten free toast and sugar free preserves.

In the beginning, when Harry, their multi-millionaire wine merchant neighbour brought home his new wife, Aline, after one of his regular business trips to Brazil, Maude thought the woman was probably an air-head, naive and totally without guile.

But as she got to know her, Maude came to appreciate just how tricky it was for someone who was so beautiful and whose figure was perfect in every way and who had started life in a poor family, to suddenly live in a world of such wealth and privilege.

Aline came to Maude's most mornings after her run and after she had showered and dressed into her day clothes, and Maude discovered the real Aline and suddenly an unusual sort of maternal instinct kicked in.

The two loved seeing each other and Maude took an ever greater protective stance in Aline's defence, even when Aline admitted that Maude's husband Gareth regularly lead her beneath a little bridge or into a secluded wooded area of the park where he would pull down her knickers and give her a quick shafting before the next part of their run.

Whether it was the loving way that Aline held Maude's hand and rubbed herself with it, or her squeezing of Maude's shoulders while she kissed her neck, Maude fell under Aline's loving spell and the two women became ever closer.

If anything, Maude felt closer to Aline on receipt of this information about her husband, secretly hoping that Gareth's regular taking advantage of Aline was being done with care and sensitivity.

"Aline, from what little I know of you, I would guess that you do enjoy erotic encounters? Am I right? And you must be constantly propositioned. Is that a problem for you, darling or do you welcome such opportunities?"

Aline thought for a moment.

"I grew up in a poor area in a notorious favela in Rio de Janeiro.

"If my early years were different to most young woman it was because of the wonderful women around me all of whom protected me, be they my older sisters, my aunts and neighbours as well as my dear mother, of course and not forgetting my two wonderful grand-mothers.

"I began to realise that I was regarded as someone special and soon discovered that I was to be raised as a virgin.

"This didn't alleviate my desire for physical contact and it wasn't long before my world was turned upside down.

I had begun secretly meeting up with two young men from college and it didn't take much persuading before they led me behind the wall of the science lab and encouraged me to suck their cocks. I loved it and wanted more. But then I was sprung and all hell let loose.

Only a day after my short but meaningful moments of sexual enlightenment behind the wall ended, my mother took me aside and told me that I would be going to stay with distant relatives, Tiago and Bibiana, wealthy wine merchants who lived down in a big and proper house in the city.

"They will teach you new things and will find you a wealthy husband, and while you remain a virgin, you might even get chosen to enter the Miss Brazil beauty pageant. We are very fortunate to have such people in the family."

Maude squeezed Alina's hand and smiled sympathetically.

"So, was this a terrible thing for you, Aline. Were your relatives good to you? Did everything work out?"

Aline gave Maude a mischievous look and smiled.

I couldn't have wished for a better situation than what eventuated. Both of my relatives were very attractive and I immediately fell into a sexual threesome with them.

It began when Bibiana showed me to my beautiful bedroom. I had hardly put down my case and removed my coat before she came up behind me and put her arms around me. She fondled my breasts and whispered gently that she hoped I would fit in and be happy in their care.

At that moment I just couldn't stop myself putting my arms back and around my aunt and pulling her firmly against my backside and gyrating against her.

"Bibiana gasped and suddenly I was laying on the bed with the head of my first woman lover under my dress, pulling my knickers off and then kissing and sucking me and finally pushing her fingers up into me and rubbing my clitoris with her thumb.

I experienced a wonderful orgasm and I was in heaven.

"As aunt Bibiana straightened her clothing, she smiled and told me that her husband would be teaching me a few important things about sex over the next day of so and said she would be with him and that I should not be frightened. Then Bibiana left saying dinner would be served downstairs at six thirty."

Maude and Aline stared at one another, both realising that they were now really horny and nothing could stop them touching each other.

Aline leant forward, pushing her mouth towards Maude and

suddenly the two hungry women had fallen onto the carpet. Each scrambled to put their heads between the others legs.

"Oh yes, Maude, stick your fingers in me Maude. Make me your slave. I so want sex with you so give it to me, please."

When the two women at last sat up and started to organise themselves, Maude kissed Aline on the cheek.

"So did you learn some important things, darling. Perhaps you could teach me some of them?"

Aline laughed out loud.

"I did, Maude. Tiago and Bibiana showed me how I could have sex without getting pregnant. Bear in mind, I was not on the pill and may family wanted me to remain a virgin.

"Bibiana called me into her room after dinner one evening. She kissed me and told me that her husband would join us shortly. Then she asked me to bend over the bed. I did so and she removed my knickers. Then I felt her playing with my bum cheeks and then I felt something being pushed into me and then Bibiana squirted lubricant into my anus.

"All this was quite mysterious but I found it exciting. Then Bibiana told me that men could put their penises into a girls bottom instead of her pussy, and they could cum in there without the girl getting pregnant.

"This was big news to me but I was apprehensive and asked what Tiago was going to do to me and she laughed."

"What do you think darling? With a bum as beautiful as yours, how will he not want to have it?

At that moment, Tiago came in and stared at me bent over the bed.

"She needs to suck me first so she has a better idea of what she will get in the back."

Tiago removed his trousers. Then he sat me up and waved his very big beautiful cock at me and told me to put it in my mouth.

Getting approval to suck a cock was the last thing I expected and I took no time at all to load it all into my mouth, excitedly sliding it around and pressing it gently with my teeth.

But then he removed it and Bibiana asked me to lay belly down on the bed again and to push my bum out towards her husband.

Feeling his hands around my waist and Bibiana holding and rubbing his cock between my buttocks felt so good and I waited excitedly, and when Tiago slowly pushed into me, my bum hole opened up like magic and engulfed him.

With confirmation of my being comfortable, Paulo began to shag me, slowly at first but then faster.

Bibiana laughed and told me what a good girl I was taking her husbands cock in my arse so easily. I looked back over my shoulder at her and smiled and told her how it felt really good. Then she said that she was happy that I was enjoying it because I would be getting a lot of it in the future.

I loved it. Suddenly I was feeling like a real woman pleasuring a man and myself. After only a short time, Paulo yelled out and squirted all of his cum up into me, then he fell forward onto me and Bibiana kissed me, then him. It was all so wonderful. I loved it and I loved them.

Maude couldn't stop herself pulling Aline to her and kissing her and the young woman responded by pushing Maude over and groping her wobbly buttocks.

"So, Aline? Did life get better for you in your aunt and uncles house? What happened next?"

Well, talk among family members continued about the possibility of me becoming a contestant in the Miss Brazil beauty pageant and eventually Tiago and Bibiana announced that they had entered me for the event and that now the big task was raising the money to pay for my making my way to the top.

I had no idea how this all worked but I was soon to find out.

"We're having our first fund raising dinner next Saturday, Aline. I hope you enjoy it. You will be the star and naturally the centre of attention. I'll help you dress for the occasion. You will need to look stunning so that you attract a lot of money."

I wasn't aware of what happened at beauty pageant fund raising events. Fortunately, one of the housemaids, Camilia, who I was very close to, told me. I was shocked at first but then I resigned myself to just do what ever was required of me.

"What did Camilia say, Aline?"

Well, it seems that there will be a bowl placed in the middle of the table. Then the wealthiest men throw large wads of money into it and in return they are entitled to have immediate access to my backside, right there and then at the table. The only condition is that they cannot ejaculate, this regulation being a tradition of some sort to support the idea of my virginity.

After they have had their way–amidst a lot of cheering from the other guests, including their wives–the men sit down and the wives take care of them, usually from underneath the table.

Licking a contestants juices off their husband cock is part of the tradition and regarded by the women as good luck. Sucking their partners off was also a favourite pastime and not just for the men who had me but all of the men. It appears that once things got started, everyone got excited and a sort of group grope and fellatio cock-fest celebration gets underway. It can get quite noisy beneath the table as women enjoy themselves, often swapping cocks and of course, touching each other up.

Maude leant forward and kissed Aline who responded with a fondling of Maude between her legs.

"So how did you go, darling. Was it difficult or did you enjoy it?"

I loved it from the word go.

A small table covered with a soft quilt was brought to stand behind my chair and only moments after the first wad of money hit the bowl, and my aunt had lifted me from my seat and bent me over and lubed my bum, I was comfortably rewarding my first financial supporter with exactly what he'd expected to get for his money.

After that it got better and better, and I gave up counting cocks. I was also excited by the sounds coming from under the table, knowing that I was being tasted and enjoyed by my bum fuckers nearest and dearest.

Then there were men yelling as their dutiful partners excitedly performed their wifely duties. I learnt later that it was not always their wife who gave them relief but often a mouth of a woman who had done a deal out of sight beneath the table, swapping cocks just for fun.

"Oh my God, Aline. What a wonderful story. But how did you end up in Sydney, sweetheart? What happened?"

Well it was to be the third fund raising dinner and I knew I was going to do well. Word from my friend Camilia, had it that we were well ahead of my opposition in fund raising and most likely in popularity too.

A few days before this third dinner, a visitor appeared and joined the family for an evening meal. His name was Harry and he was from Australia and a big customer of Tiago's wine business. He was staying at a top hotel close by and was shortly due to return to Sydney.

He seemed very nice and obviously he was a man who knew what he wanted.

Camilia told me in strictest confidence that he visited twice a year. More importantly, she told how on the first occasion, Tiago noticed Harry's infatuation with his wife and in loving consultation with Bibiana, had offered Harry her backside, telling him it was the finest in the land.

Bibiana had not objected and laughed and in fact welcomed her husbands praise along with Harry's interest.

"I would love you to have it right now, Senhor. Come with me to the dormitòrio."

Camilia also told me how Tiago and she had followed shortly after and peeped at the two.

She said how Harry was giving Bibiana a gigantic anal shagging which made Camilia turn to Tiago and smile and reach out to him and that the two had gone back into the dinning room where he tore off her clothes, dragging her and fucking her all around the house.

I think Camilia might have enjoyed exaggerating but it made a good story.

Anyway! To shorten the story, it seems that Harry, after his moments with Bibiana's rear end, was totally sold on Brazilian women's backsides.

He made an extraordinary offer to my aunt and uncle for my hand in marriage and after a day or more of haggling within my family, my prospects as the wife of a wealthy man seemed greater than those of a would-be beauty queen and we were married in a small suburban church and enjoyed the traditional wedding celebrations with much dancing and wonderful food.

The following day we left for Australia and bingo! Here I am.

The two stopped talking and Maude seemed deep in thought. Then Aline laughed and said, "I know what you're thinking and yes I need to tell you everything."

When we arrived home in Australia, we still hadn't really consummated the marriage other than a quick fumble in the vestry straight after the ceremony. Harry had just opened his trousers and I was about to suck him when we were interrupted.

So when we arrived home late morning and after Harry had shown me around the house I was expecting something might happen but it didn't, at least not until the evening.

When evening came, my husband led me upstairs to a small room where some clothes were laid out on a bed and he asked me to put them on and that he would return shortly.

I was confused but I did as he asked.

The clothes seemed a bit old fashioned but in a nice way. Brown stockings with seams and beige knickers and bra and a suspender belt. The top was a simple soft silky cream fabric and the tight skirt was wool and brown and it had a zipper in the back. Low heeled brown shoes made up the outfit. He had also asked me to put my hair back in a bun, even providing a brown ribbon. As I enjoyed doing all of this I wondered just what was going to be the result.

When Harry came through the door, he just stood and stared at me. Then he smiled and came over to me and kissed me lovingly on the lips and then he turned me around very slowly and began to unzip my skirt. It fell to the floor around my feet and I felt his eyes staring at me in my stockings and knickers and suspenders.

Harry's gentle onslaught of my more than willing body took us both to heaven and back and then back to heaven again. Harry couldn't get enough of my bum and I couldn't get enough of Harry's beautiful big cock. And when he finally exploded inside me and slowly slid out of me, I rolled over and put him in my mouth and lay beside him, clutching his testicles and murmuring loving words.

I knew that what Harry had given me was the best anal sex I would ever experience and I loved him for it.

But then came the bombshell. Harry then told me that he would never want to make love to my vagina. He said he was perfectly happy with my bottom and asked if I would dress in those clothes late each afternoon before he came home from work.

He could see that I was perplexed and he fondled my hair and smiled and kissed me.

Then came the second bombshell.

"You are free, dear wife, to have sex with your vagina with whomever you please. The one simple request is that never, under any circumstances offer your backside to another man. It belongs to me. Do you understand?"

I couldn't answer him. I just stared and then I began to cry. "I've been a virgin for too long Harry!" I cried. "You can't do this to me. It's cruel."

He took my hand then he embraced me. "I just told you, darling, that you are free to do whatever you like with your beautiful pussy. In fact I believe I know how to get you started in a way that you will enjoy. I'll talk to you about it again in the morning. Now, dry your eyes."

Maude held Aline close and wiped a tear from her cheek.

"Why would a man do that? I just don't understand. Then what happened?"

Aline sat up and sniffled and then she smiled and said how she suddenly remembered something sexual she'd witnessed at one of the fund raising dinners and which she found interesting.

It was towards the end of the contribution of my backside to my paying benefactors.

Uncle Tiago had just resumed his seat at the table when suddenly, his sister-in-law, Luiza, threw herself onto the table in front of him. She rolled on her back and let her head fall over the edge of the table, almost in Tiago's lap while yelling, "fuck me cara!"

Then she proceeded to liberate his very rigid cock from his pants, dragging it all the way down into her big upside down mouth.

Tiago stood up and proceeded to energetically fuck her mouth while all the time, the woman rubbed herself between her legs. When he shot his load, the woman orgasmed and only moments later she was sitting at the table helping herself to a desert and acting as though nothing had happened.

What they had done appealed to me in some odd way and as Harry finished talking, I made my demand.

"If you are having my bum exclusively, darling, then I want something exclusive to us."

Harry stared at me and asked, "What do you suggest, Aline?"

"I want you to face-fuck me sometimes, and to promise that you will never do it with anyone else."

Maude looked shocked. "But you hadn't even found out if you liked it or not?"

"I know. Maybe I was a bit hasty. But then Harry gave me his serene smile and suggested we do it there and then. I couldn't really say no as I was the one suggesting it. So we did."

Maude continued to look shocked. "And …"

I loved it. Harry was quite gentle. He laid me on the kitchen table so that my head hung over the side. I directed him between my lips and teeth while I touched myself and Harry tugged my nipples a bit and after only a short time, we both happily exploded with me managing not to bite off his cock.

Harry and I both laughed and hugged one another and Harry asked me if that was good enough to be my exclusive demand of him. I told him that it would do very nicely and that I would expect him to give it to me on demand as I did for him when he wanted my bum. And I added that I might want him to practice sometimes.

"So everything turned out for the best darling? Now I will want to know how you ended up with my husband, but I have an appointment shortly so that delicious morsel of information will just have to wait.

Oh before you go, there is more to tell you but it can wait. Bibiana had to teach me about male masturbation, and that was just super exciting.

Darling, I just can't wait to hear, but later. I must dash.

What Maude failed to mention to Aline was that she had promised her friend and guest, Gwen, a Wednesday lunchtime visit to the dogging venue at the Golf Club.

"You might not get what you wanted like you would on a Friday night, Gwen, but I know you won't be happy until you've shown yourself off, so get into the Merc and we'll give it a go."

Gwen was visibly excited and fell into the passenger seat alongside Maude.

"Oh God, Maude? I'm wet already, just thinking about it."

The woman wriggled about trying to get comfortable in her tighter-than-tight skirt.

When they arrived, Maude drove in quite a distance and parked beneath some trees in a small carpark overlooking the ocean. The weather was mild and balmy.

Half a dozen cars were already parked and Maude noticed that at least half of them had a woman in the drivers seat and each was either alone or with another female. "Lonely, Horney wives at midday, each looking for an adventure that would'nt upset their lives."

The other cars were empty, suggesting that the driver was already occupied somewhere in the bushes.

Maude thought about that woman in the bushes who might be having her first moment of something different and she envied her. Oh for those exciting first moments with another man's cock after years with her poor boring husband. Enjoy it, my dear and help yourself to more. You will never regret it and ultimately, neither will your husband.

"I think we'll have a bit of competition, Gwen. But not to worry," she laughed. "Quality always wins out."

Gwen laughed and said how she would love to go and inspect the opposition but she probably shouldn't.

Maude reached across and rubbed the top of her friends stockinged leg, letting her fingers poke beneath Gwen's suspender. Gwen gave a little squeal and whispered that that was a good start and that it had increased her state of randiness.

"If we don't get any takers, Maude, could we hop in the back together?"

Maude smiled back. "I promise you will get something better, darling. Just undo your top and show a nipple. That gets them going."

Maude moved into the back of the big old car and made herself comfortable. She leisurely removed her skirt and her knickers and opened her top, displaying her super impressive breasts, a present her husband had paid for the Christmas before last. Then she flicked her large nipples enjoying the feel of them rubbing against the silicon beneath. Maude knew that they would attract any man's mouth.

Then she wriggled down into the comfy seat and opened her legs and admired them as they reached up towards her modest tuft of public hair. Then she palmed her pussy. Maude adjusted her masquerade mask and whispered to herself, "I'm ready boys."

Then she opened the door wide to give a good view of her long shapely legs and her sexy laid-back body.

With the door open and the winter sun on her semi naked frame, Maude lay back and closed her eyes and fantasised about moments she'd enjoyed in the past. Then Gwen called out from the front seat.

"Oh my God, I've got two!"

"Just don't rush darling. They will appreciate you more if you relax and take your time."

Gwen didn't answer and when Maude opened one eye to see what was happing on the front seat, Gwen had a large cock in her hand and another in her mouth and two arms were busy feeling between her legs.

In what seemed no time at all, Gwen was out of the car and being led away along a little path into the treed woodland. Daylight dogging protocol required people to hide in the bushes, unlike under the cover of darkness when anything goes and when some women discovered a sensual or sexual side of themselves they didn't know they had, simply by getting out of the car and moving onto the lawn.

Gwen's short skirt was already up around her waist and two mens hands held and fondled her adequate buttocks, supposedly to help stop her falling off of her high heels.

Then Maude notice three men already lurking near the path

leading into the woods and Maude hoped that Gwen would be treated well. She reasoned that if this was to be Gwen's first gang bang, doing it in the light of day was probably safer. And unlike pubic dogging venues, this was a safe spot, regulated so that any complaints about bad behaviour resulted in expulsion from the club.

Maude lay quietly soaking up the sun and thinking that for her, it had been a long time between gang bangs. She thought how that might be something she'd put on her list for next week.

Then Maude heard a sound and only partly opened her eyes, sufficient to see a very large and beautiful thick cock waving at her from the doorway. Maude willingly took hold of it and stroked it gently and rubbed it without even looking up at the owner.

Very quickly, she put it into her mouth and began to savour it and entertain herself, and hopefully, the owner. She felt those thousands of tiny sensors in her genitals wake up and lead her slowly towards becoming more demonstrative and eager to satisfy her ever present sexual hunger.

It was only when she peeped through her mask to see if the man on the end of the lovely cock was enjoying himself that she saw who it was. Maude was shocked.

The man was her next-door neighbour, Harry whose beautiful wife, Aline, Maude was licking and fingering just an hour earlier. How was this possible? Surely he got enough of what he wanted at home?

Then Maude began to think of the details of what Aline had described that Harry gave her each night before bed and suddenly, Maude felt a twinge in her pussy and she knew exactly what she wanted.

Without a second thought, Maude let go of Harry's cock and swivelled around onto her belly and moved backwards until the high heels on the ends of her long legs touched the ground.

Then, she quickly searched around and found the lube and reached back and parted her buttocks and squirted liquid into her bum hole. Then lifted her backside up and moved it provocatively in front of Harry.

Maude had made it obvious to him what she wanted and prayed that he would give it to her. Anal sex was the thing that gave Maude the most joy in life and she regretted that her husband had never embraced it.

Maude heard Harry chuckle.

"Well, it's not often I score an anal slut or perhaps I should say an anal angel. It must be my lucky day. Hopefully, I'll make it hers too."

Harry rotated his large hands on Maude's bare buttocks and squeezed them in appreciation, telling her that her arse was the most beautiful he'd seen in a long time.

Harry took Maude to heaven. For more than half an hour the two met each heave and thrust of Harry's giant cock. Maude moaned and sometimes pleaded for more of something to which Harry responded with a most craftsman-like performance.

Maude easily imagined herself being Aline and standing in her brown stockings and other stuff to get Harry's attention each night before bed and when she did, her body shuddered.

It was as they were coming to the end of their lovemaking and Maude had orgasmed many times, that her womanly wiles kicked in and Maude began to plan how she would get her friend's husband Harry into her rear end again or even to give it to her on a regular basis.

Maude figured that she and Aline could now happily share their husbands with each other.

When Harry yelled and filled Maude's orifice with his cum, Maude lay resting then she turned and, as she slowly removed her mask and smiled at her neighbour she whispered, "Thank you, Harry". Please visit me any time you want it. I'll be very happy for you to enjoy my arse any time of the day or night.

Harry looked shocked at first but then, as things became apparent in his mind, he quickly smiled back.

"Where and when will I find you, Maude?"

Maude fondled Harry's large and now flaccid cock.

How about the first Wednesday of each month, at around this time? It will save us both driving up to the Golf Course.

"I keep this old car in the big shed at the back of the garden. We'd both love to see you there. I'll open that little gate in the fence. Say you will come, Harry?"

"I'll be there, Maude. I promise."

———————

After Harry had left, Maude made herself comfortable, to await her girlfriends return from her adventure.

An hour or more had passed since Gwen left the car and Maude figured that she would give her a full hour and half before going in search of her.

It wasn't unheard of that sometimes, woman temporarily would pass out and be left alone, their dogging lovers thinking the woman was simply resting and hopefully to be discovered by a friend in a little while.

In the fading light, a figure suddenly appeared out of the tea-tree. Gwen wandered slowly towards the Merc a little uncertain on her bare feet.

Maude jumped from the car and went to meet her.

"Gwen! Are you all right darling. Is everything okay, sweetheart? Talk to me."

Gwen stopped and stared at Maude heading towards her. Then she smile a far-away smile.

"Oh yes, darling. I'm fine. In fact I'm more than fine."

Maude took Gwen's arm and led her to the car and popped her into the back seat on the old beach towel and got in beside her then put her arms around her friend.

"Now, Gwen. The truth, please? Are you sure you are really okay? I'm taking you home for a nice hot bath and then putting you straight to bed."

Gwen reached forward and pulled Maude close and looked for her lips.

"Kiss me Maude. Make love to me. I want you, you gorgeous woman. Feel how I'm still orgasming? You must feel it darling, I want to share them with you."

Maude was indeed feeling the large tremors that went through her friends body ever minute or two. It was quite odd but it did feel good.

Maude looked closely at Gwen and saw that her eyes were glazed and not really focused. Then Gwen grabbed Maude's hand and pulled it in between her legs.

Maude thought how it was she who was still wet. Harry's contribution to her bum was still leaking out. But her hand discovered Gwen's saturated hairy cunt, and when she felt behind her, she found that Gwen had obviously had many visits between her buttocks as well.

Maude disentangled herself from her desperately horny friend, telling her that they would be home in just twelve minutes and to please not move until then.

Gwen sat back on the towel, rubbing herself and having an orgasm every few minutes.

"I'm so pleased to see you, Maude," is all Gwen kept saying apart from yelling "Yes" whenever she came.

It was when Maude had Gwen safely in the big bath that she began to see what she had been through. And it added up to quite a picture in Maude's mind. There were bite marks all over her; her breast, her belly, her thighs, her shoulders, her back and her bum. Some were already turning a shadowy blue.

When Maude lathered her friends pussy, Gwen screamed "Oh yes!" then she threw her arms around Maude and screamed for more, then shuddered with a huge orgasm.

Maude had never seen anything quite like it before. Part of her was very worried but then the only stress Gwen was really showing was that she simply wanted more sex.

Gwen grabbed Maude's soapy hands and rubbed them on her belly and her breasts. Then she looked at Maude with pleading in her eyes and begged her to take her to bed and fuck her with Maud's biggest dildo.

"I love that big black fucker you've got hidden in the bottom draw, Maude. I want it right up me. Say you'll give it to me, Maude."

If this was some sort of delirium, then Maude was uncertain what she should do. Bringing her friend down to a semblance of rational thinking was her priority. She wasn't sure the dildo idea was a good one although it momentarily appealed to her.

Maude was thinking furiously. Then she had an idea. It was a long shot but it might work.

"Well, we could, but I've planned a wonderful meal and was looking forward to us sharing it. Roast crispy chicken and roast potato's and vegetables followed by pavlova and supreme creamy vanilla ice cream. And I've bought lychees. I know you love them.

Maude stared in amazement as Gwen's face changed and suddenly, in a most normal voice she said, "Yes please, darling. And do we have a bottle of runny cream in the fridge? Now that would make my day."

Suddenly, Gwen's world had changed. No longer were her eyes glazed or her speech slightly incoherent. And she stopped shuddering. And she simply ran some more hot water then picked up the soap and washed between her legs and buttocks and laughingly told Maude that it had been a good day and that she had really enjoyed it.

It was now Maude who was in a state of shock. She just thanked her maker that she had planned this meal in advance with her lovely home help.

It was Mrs Maitland housekeeping day and she had agreed to cook, and yes, Maude had put a bottle of runny cream on the shopping list.

Over the next few days, nothing much was said about Gwen's adventure except that she complained about her bruises as though they just arrived mysteriously out of the blue.

Maude thought a lot about what had happened and she tried to make sense of it all. Gwen seemed just fine and they never ever discussed that memorable dogging adventure.

All she learnt from Gwen was that she had loved every minute of her time with those men on Wednesday.

Maude would remember that day forever and never stop wondering what happened. And not knowing would always be a question mark in her encyclopaedic understanding of dogging.

But then as she was often heard to say, "A girl can't know everything."

NINETEEN

MORE ADVENTURES OF ALINE

It was their first meeting after Maude had enjoyed Aline's husband Harry, at the dogging site.

Maude had decided not to mention it at this stage. It could stay a secret for a bit longer, at least until she could weave the story into a reasonable narrative.

She was also uncertain about mentioning that she had met Harry while he was dogging. Aline might find his dogging activity was not to her liking and an insult to her wifely mission.

"Hello darling! So good to see you. Lets kiss a bit. I missed you yesterday."

Aline was full of beans and delightfully loving and they kissed and touched each other.

"Now, Maude, darling. Do you want me to continue my story from when I was still at my aunt and uncles place? I've told you most but then I remembered I'd missed a bit. Would you like to hear about it?"

"Of course I do, you sexy little bitch. But what more could you possibly have gotten up to?"

They both made themselves a coffee then Aline settled back and began to tell Maude her story.

"It must have been a few weeks before I met Harry. Bibiana popped into my room one morning and said there was something she and Tiago had forgotten to talk to me about and that she was now organising for me to get fully up to date."

Being a virgin was all very well, she said, but like all things it carried responsibilities to ensure that people were happy.

She told me that ways to make men happy included masturbating them. This would also take the pressure off you needing to provide access to your rear end all the time, she told me. Then she added, or them trying to climb in between your legs and not respecting your virginal status.

It sounds strange but my weird virgin upbringing had left me hopelessly ignorant about what most people would see as ordinary and obvious.

She tried to tell me how men ejaculated but it didn't make a lot of sense to me and she though about that.

While I loved men rubbing themselves inside my bum it had not taught me much because at the rules of fund raising, all of the men withdrew before they had their big moment, withdrawing, and then turning to their wives to complete the task.

Then Bibiana said that the best way to learn was by practice and that she would arrange something just for that purpose.

Bibiana's side of the family had young men studying for the priesthood or in some cases, already young priests.

I had come from a background of poverty where the church played only a small part in our day to day lives, simply being there to help the parishioners.

Things were very different in the city where morals didn't always match up with real life social activity, or was never much restrained.

Bibiana called me into the spare bedroom one afternoon and introduced me to two young trainee Dominicans'; brothers who the family had expected to become priests.

"Aline? This is Pedro and Carlos." They nodded and smiled.

Then Bibiana walked over to the two young men and smiled and asked them to remove their over-shirts and tunics.

I watched with great interest and was quickly confronted with two well hung young men whose large healthy cocks seemed to twitch and turn the more I stared at them. I was enthralled.

"Now Aline? One each! Just follow me. Masturbating men isn't that hard."

Bibiana took me by the hand and together we knelt down on the carpet and she showed me how to take hold of a cock and play with it.

I loved it.

"Now darling, just hold it close to the testicles and then move your hand along it and back and along it and back. And when it starts to get big and hard, you can start popping it in and out of your mouth and licking or even sucking it."

I was simply over the moon with this new activity. Rarely had I been allowed to even get my hands on a cock. Bibiana's Tiago had been one but then it was only for a short time and I was very frustrated when he stopped me.

I Looked across at my aunt who was now busy slurping away at Carlos's cock while I was gingerly touching and nervously tugging at Pedro.

I suddenly heard Carlo make excited noises and I looked over just as Bibiana dragged his cock deep into her mouth and made him cum there.

Bibiana looked over at me, her mouth seemingly filled with something.

"There, darling. I've caught his cum in my mouth and made him happy at the same time. I've masturbated him! Now tug and rub and suck Pedro and see what you can do. I promise you will enjoy it."

I eventually did succeed with Pedro and after he had yelled and cum and then wandered off to get dressed, I sat back on my legs and rolled his cum around in my mouth.

"Well, done darling," Bibiana called out from across the room. "I'll get them back again tomorrow and you can practice some more."

Over the next week, I played with ten different cocks on multiple days, all belonging to young members or friends of Bibiana's family.

At the end of that time, I was beginning to get the hang of things and by the time I had been through all of them at least three times, I prided myself that I could masturbate a cock and get it to cum within five minutes or less.

Bibiana was very pleased with me.

"Now you can enjoy cocks, my love. As many as you want. I suspect by what I've seen that you will want plenty. Am I right, Aline?"

I smiled at her and answered.

"Oh, yes auntie, I will want plenty. I think sucking cocks is going to become my hobby. I just love them. And any help you can offer will be much appreciated."

TWENTY

MORE THAN ENOUGH

It was Thursday, the day ofter Maude's lunchtime dogging session with her friend Gwen, and her heavenly encounter with her neighbour, Harry. Aline was due to visit at any moment and Maude was feeling both nervous and excited.

Maude was feeling invigorated after her memorable moments with Aline's husband and she now felt an unexplainable hunger for Harry's beautiful wife.

Aline arrived and stared lovingly at Maude. Then she crossed the room and sat on Maude's knee and embraced her and kissed her on the lips. Aline was exhibiting signs of hunger, too.

Maude responded and it felt as though great minds were coming together and an explosion was about to happen. Was this some sort of after effect from Maude's recent experience with Harry? Was Aline picking up some sort of sexual vibration? Or was it something else?

Aline hung her arms around Maude's neck and covered her with wet kisses. Then she reached down and slipped her hand up Maude's skirt.

"Maude, darling? I have dreams, fantasies I suppose. Part of me misses what I got from those men at my fund raiser sessions back in San Paulo. I sometimes wake up thrusting myself up and down, imagining I'm on my belly back then on the table and them all having me, one after the other. I want you to help me."

"I'm so horny, Maude. I want you to get out your biggest dildo and fuck my bum. Ravage me. Please! Please!

"And when you've finished inside me, suck and lick my juices off the big cock, just like those mens wives did. It will be so good knowing that you did that, Maude."

It took only a few moments for Maude to find and fasten the buckle on her biggest black rubber cock.

"Oh, Maude. Yes, darling. That is exactly what I want," Aline croaked excitedly as she ran her fingers up and down the dildo.

Aline took off her knickers and went and laid over the arm of the settee and Maude applied lubricant between the woman's perfect buttocks.

Then Maude mounted Aline and grunted like an excited male and the two woman gasped and panted and then they ceremoniously screamed and yelled while Maude relentlessly shafted the welcoming backside of the woman she was now totally in love with.

Maude called Aline names and said silly things. "You dirty whore! You anal slut! Your brains live in her backside and from now on I'll only talk to your bum."

Eventually, Aline screamed and came and Maude followed suit, then the two fell onto the carpet and held each other tight, kissing and murmuring sweet things. Then Aline sat back and watched as Maude closed her eyes and lovingly licked Aline's juices off of the dildo.

"Thank you for fucking me like that, Maude. Everything is so much better now. I love you more than anything or anyone.

Maude smothered Aline with kisses and then the two sat back against the settee and thought about their new world.

———

Last time we were together, you were planning to tell me how you and Gareth got together. How did that happen, darling?

"Ah, yes, Maude. I was telling you how Harry was going to organise for me to lose my virginity, wasn't I?"

Harry has friends who operate a fitness centre just a few streets away and he enrolled me in their fun run program.

"What I didn't know was that the fun runs were simply a front for people to get out and discover each other. And I don't mean simply a "get to know you" discovery but more a "would you like to fuck me?" get together.

"On the first day, one of the staff, a woman named Tina, led me and two men on a jogging event in Centennial Park. As it happened, your husband Gareth was one of the men. A man named George was the other one.

"I later found out that Harry had suggested to Gareth that he should enrol to make sure I was "looked after".

"Half way along the route, Tania led us off the main track into a thicket of bushes. Then she turned and smiled at us as she pulled down her shorts and knickers, saying out loud, "I think we should stop for a bit of cock. Now boys! Who wants to be first?"

"I watched in amazement as first, George exposed his rapidly rising member and offered it to Tania, who took hold of it and dropped to her knees and began to suck him.

"Then your Gareth let his penis out and that was the beginning of the end for both of us.

"I fell to my knees and pulled him into my mouth, excited beyond belief that I was at last being let loose with adults doing stuff I'd only recently been practicing before arriving in Australia. But it didn't stop just with sucking.

"Tania stood up and pushed her fluffy pussy at George's face and told him to fuck her and he did. As the two settled into a serious shagging mode, Gareth asked me if I wanted to be fucked standing or kneeling. Without stopping to think about it, I replied that kneeling sounded like a good way to start, and that is what we did. It was so good.

"I lost my virginity at that moment and haven't looked back.

I now set off with Gareth and I get him to give it to me quite soon, usually in a favourite alleyway not far from home.

"Then we get joined by other joggers most of whom seem to know what is going on and a little while later, we head into the bushes, and while Gareth enjoys a couple of new ladies, I can sometimes get up to four or more lovely cocks, all of whom I lovingly suck and then slide into my wet pussy. I then enjoying orgasming and being filled with cum. It is so lovely."

Maude held Aline close and kissed her. Then the young woman lifted up her teeshirt and pulled Maude's face to her breasts while at the same time she explored Maude's super shapely breasts and rubbed her nipples.

"Maude? I've wanted to ask you something for quite a while."

"Yes, darling, ask me anything you like."

"I know you say you are okay with the me and Gareth thing, but I wonder about it, and I wonder if you are getting the attention you would like in life.

"You've never mentioned anybody else and I want to know if you're being truly looked after? Be honest with me Maude. Do you really get enough loving in your life?"

Maude squeezed Aline's hand while thinking just how special this young woman was.

"As we get older, things change. My relationship with my husband changed a long time ago and it is just as well it did.

"My freedom to do whatever I want with whoever I want is the single most important thing. I can have a very active sex life if I want to or I can relax and enjoy different things if and when I feel the need.

"An example is that Gareth and I would never make love by choice but we have an arrangement which is both silly and fun.

"When Gareth gave me breast enhancement surgery as a present, he was selfishly doing it for himself. But that didn't matter to me.

"I just have fun once a week after our Sunday afternoon nap. I call out from my bedroom informing him that his valuable Assets need moisturising.

"Gareth immediately jumps on me and energetically shags me, and then at the last moment he pulls his cock out and ejaculates all over my tits.

"He loves to watch me spreading his cum all over me, claiming he was told it will keep my tits young for ever.

"But you mustn't worry about a thing, Aline. I have a number of women friends who I enjoy doing things with. Each friend enjoys different things so that I have an endless choice of sexual adventures.

"I'm a member of the Golf club and like many women, I spend a lot of time at exclusive dogging sites around the club and enjoy multiple men and sometimes women. It's not unlike what you experience when jogging, I suppose.

"I regularly meet up with a couple of women I've got to know at the club and we will have fun dogging together, playing with one another as each of us also entertain a number of men. It is great fun. We've discovered we can multi-task even when dogging.

"I'm also a member of the Sydney Swingers Club and I can experience many sexual fun things there when ever I get the urge.

"Please don't worry about me in any way, darling. I promise I'm just fine and my sensual life is very full. But thank you."

The most recent man's offering from just a moment ago, ran out of both sides of Maude's mouth and oozed down her chin from where it dribbled and dripped onto her already cum covered breasts.

"That was lovely! Thank you. Please call on me again."

This was Maude's common farewell as gratified men returned themselves to their trousers and left.

Maude now held the next man's beautiful cock in her hand and stared at it lovingly, then she smiled up through the open window.

"Thank you. This looks lovely."

Then she put out her tongue and licked the moist spot from the end of his bright red knob before feeding him into her mouth.

For Maude, this was life at its very best. The weather was good and a plentiful supply of men, hungry for her mouth just kept arriving.

Maude had ventured out for just a few moments to show herself off and that was enough to keep her busy for the rest of the afternoon. She wore her tight skirt and stockings and heels on her daylight dogging adventures; and she only had to drop the skirt part the way down around her knees to get the attention she wanted. It only worked in daylight for some reason. Friday nights crowd either couldn't see what she wore or did or were not particularly interested.

Maude wiped her fingers on her sticky chest then reached down and rubbed cum on to her vagina and touched her clitoris.

It was getting quite late in the evening and the mellow carpark lights were making it more difficult to read peoples faces. But that didn't matter. The men knew what they wanted and Maude knew even better, what they needed.

Soon, her friend Belinda in the late model people-carrier two cars back, would text her and Maude would close her window and turn her car and park it behind Belinda. Moving the car was a simple procedure to signal that she had closed for the evening.

When Maude arrived at the door of Belinda's van, she knocked in a special way and her friend quickly slid open the big side door and dragged her in. Then both woman fell onto the mattress on the floor and laughed delightedly, enjoying each others company after a busy afternoon.

They would often start by licking each others breasts, ostensibly to savour the accumulated cum, but they both knew that it was really just a teaser for the nipple sucking and bosom fondling that they both loved.

"My God Belinda, it must be nearly thirty years since we first got our mouths on each others tits, and each time feels as exciting as that first time."

Belinda removed her mouth and sighed.

"Oh yes, darling, I remember that moment so well. How could I forget it? Our boyfriends had drunk to much and didn't make it to the car. We simply looked at each other and then you climbed into the back seat with me. We knew that we wanted to touch each other, and we did. It was so good."

"Yes, and you being the slut you were, pulled my hand up under your skirt and made me finger you. We discovered that playing with each other was better than pulling on our dum boyfriends cocks."

"But it wasn't just me. We pulled each others knickers down and got into a sixty-nine straight away. And most memorable was that we both came at the same time on each others sex hungry mouths. God, we were so horny for each other.

"Life was never the same after that. I so missed you when you moved to Sydney."

"I missed you too Belinda. But now, at long last we are reunited and we can enjoy gobbling cunts and cocks together again. By the way, that reminds me, will you be going to Ursula's party next Saturday night?"

"I will. I'm inviting a couple who are totally new to swinging."

"Now that will be really interesting. You shouldn't have told me, Belinda. I might be tempted to introduce myself and misbehave. I'll confide in them about our love affair and how we killed our husbands and buried them in the garden just so we could be together."

Belinda burst out laughing. "I wouldn't put it past you, you slut."

"Oh, and while I'm thinking about it, Maude, you must promise me you won't wear that old red garter belt with bows or I will never be able to spread my favours. You know damn well what it doe to me. Memories from all those years ago are still very powerful."

"Well, Belinda. If I can just remember where I put it, I'll wear it and if I'm just not getting what I want and I'm bored, I'll wander over and smile at you and lift my skirt. Will that get you chasing me into a broom cupboard and having your way with me with a brush handle?"

"Oh yes, and remind me again what happened that my garter belt got you going? What did I do that was so exciting?"

"You know damned well what happened. I simply came out of the dance hall for some fresh air and when I walked around the side, there you were leaning back agains the wall in just your red stockings and bra and strappy high heels and that bloody garter belt. You had two young men each with his cock tucked under your suspenders and poked into your stocking tops and you were gently moving, gyrating to try and get them to come on your panties and calling out "Come on boys. I know you can do it."

"Oh yes! I remember. That was a long time ago. Damned if I can remember whether it worked? I wonder what they are doing now? They might like to do it again?"

"You are such a slut. No wonder I love you so much."

And so ended another perfect day for Maude. All she could get of whatever she wanted and whenever she wanted it. Love was everywhere and life just couldn't get any better.

AFTERWORD

In a matriarchal structure, such as exists in some tribes in South India, women have natural confidence in their own womanhood. They know their importance and that they are different from men in a special way, and this does not imply any inferiority. They are able to assert their human existence and being in a natural way.

So writes Marie Louise Von Franz in her book, *The Feminine in Fairy Tales.*

One should acknowledging Lilith, known by some as the Queen of the Night and by others as the ancient bad girl.

Lilith was said to have been Adams first wife. She was not happy with him and left. Her reasons included him always making her lie beneath him when making love and also demanding her complete obedience.

Eve replaced her and later Lilith was often represented in art by the serpent. (*See the sculpture at the entrance of Notre Dame cathedral depicting Adam and Eve, and Lilith as a serpent.*)

CONTACT

Publisher or review enquiries should include your full name and details in all correspondence.

Email Address:
countrynotebook@gmail.com

RICHARD LEE PUBLISHING

Erotic Fiction

New 2022:

Wet Dreams for Oldies 1: Never feel lonely again (P/back)

ISBN: 978-0-909431-22-8

Wet Dreams for Oldies 1: Never feel lonely again (H/back)

ISBN: 978-0-909431-40-2

Wet Dreams for Oldies 2: Never feel lonely again (P/back)

ISBN: 978-0-909431-24-2

The Eros Crescent trilogy as paperbacks or ebooks:

The Fifi Code

ISBN - 978-0-909431-02-0

Eros Crescent

ISBN - 978-0-909431-05-1

Mount Eros

ISBN - 978-0-909431-08-2

Excerpts from the Eros Crescent series as paperbacks or ebooks:

Janice: A sexual enigma

ISBN - 978-0-909431-10-5

Jessica: A young woman's journey

ISBN - 978-0-909431-13-6

Helen: Enough is not enough

ISBN - 978-0-909431-14-3

Maria: Always available

ISBN - 978-0-909431-15-0

Mary: Catching up

ISBN - 978-0-909431-11-2

The Club: Ladies love it!

ISBN - 978-0-909431-11-2

Happy Honeypots: Swinging in Harmony

ISBN - 978-0-909431-20-4

Roger: Ladies love to pay him

ISBN - 978-0-909431-21-1

Literary Fiction

Australian Short Stories

ISBN - 978-0-909431-00-6

Restless: A novel about two young men growing up in Australia between 1900 and 1936 (Publication date not set.)

Out of Print Titles

Mathematics for Young Children by Helen Western

ISBN - 978-0-909431-01-3

Currajong: For Those Whom Schools Have Failed

by Bruce Wicking

ISBN - 978-0-909431-03-7

The Puppetry Handbook by Anita Sinclair

ISBN - 978-0-909431-04-4

Wordswork by Chris Davidson & Bruce Wicking

ISBN - 978-0-909431-06-8

Sheep Production by Murray Elliott

ISBN - 978-0-909431-07-5

Ducks for Starters: A Practical Guide to

Backyard Duck Keeping by Bruce Wicking

ISBN - 978-1-875207-00-8

Sweethearts by Colin Talbot

ISBN - 978-1-875207-02-2